TALON
By Lona Wilson

Dedicated to Charlotte Turnmeyer, my awesome editor.

4

Table of Contents

Chapter 1
Chapter 2
Chapter 3
Chapter 4
Chapter 5
Chapter 6
Chapter 7
Chapter 8
Chapter 9
Chapter 10
Chapter 11
Chapter 12
Chapter 13
Chapter 14
Epilog

Chapter 1

His sister-in-law looked at him with her hands on her hips and a *very* anguished face.

"I have a six-month-old baby to take care of now and don't have the time or energy to help you a second time, Talon. You didn't listen, and now you've seriously hurt your knee again. So, back you go to therapy, but this time without me as your therapist."

"Em, please. It would be so easy. We have everything here, and I wouldn't even have to leave the house." Tapping his fingers on the kitchen table, "Just think! Swimming pool, complete exercise room with every toy you can think of..."

Turning to hand Cailen to him, "Here, you take care of Cailen while I fold a few clothes. The answer is still no. If you stay around here day in and day out, then you're going to be a full-time nanny. Got it?"

"I'd make a lousy Nanny," spoke Talon. Holding Cailen up in the air and swinging him around, he listened as Emily remarked on his self-imposed exile.

"Most likely. But you probably would make a good father, oddly enough. One of these days you should consider going back to Pennsylvania and see if you are a…"

"Drop it, Em. It's not up for discussion." He narrowed his eyes and turned his face away from her while wrapping one arm around Cailen. Oh, he was a father, alright. He'd even confessed to Declan that he had at least two children that he knew of. He was lucky though. Those two women had married nice guys and the children were growing up in stable homes. Interlocking his fingers around the boy's stomach he bounced Cailen on his lap, wondering what it would have been like to bounce one of his own around like this. He was never one to think much about kids, but he had to admit he loved being an uncle to Cailen.

Standing up straight and folding her arms in front of her, Emily showed her displeasure at Talon's denial of his past. Despite his many years of self-debasement, she honestly thought it would help him heal to face it. Her husband had shared Talon's secret with her. At least two children, he had said. Talon hadn't seemed to be embarrassed by it, and hadn't sworn him to secrecy, so Em just treated it as another part of the Talon puzzle that needed to be put together. She had to drop it.

"Neither is my physical therapy degree going to help you a second time. You are going to go back to your doctor, who will give you a referral to a Therapy Network in the area – one that will take the insurance that Declan has so kindly set you up with."

"Em, please? I'm begging here."

"Nope. You are the one who went skiing at Wintergreen. You're the one who tried to ski down a hill not up to your skills, and you're the one who got that knee hurt. You heard the doctor, Talon. If you hurt that leg again you are going to limp the rest of your life. Those were bad injuries you recovered from the last time. You were very lucky." Folding the last of the little outfits, "You've done *so* well this past year. Just do it right this time and don't make the rest of your life painful."

"This knee has messed me up something fierce."

"What do you mean?"

"I had to stop working part time for the carpentry shop. I did manage to get a small savings account going, but it's barely enough. I do manage a couple hours a day at my little rented space though. I enjoy that." Leaning back into the chair, balancing Cailen on his lap, he paused and glanced around the room. A very large kitchen in a very large house. Nothing had been ignored in the planning of *this* house. More rooms than you could count. Separate wings. Dedicated television room with several lounge chairs. Watching at Cailen, sitting on his lap, facing him, he could see the Seaton face. A perfect boy who was going to grow up to be a lady killer. All the Seaton men had been gorgeous, and he had always used that to his advantage. Cailen was not going to be the exception to that rule. Even at his young age he was a handsome devil. Beautiful hazel eyes, dark hair, extremely long eyelashes, (which made Emily green with envy – she commented on it at least once a day), and even a dimple when he smiled. Emily knew how to dress him too. Today it was blue jeans and an adorable western shirt. Talon rested his chin on top of Cailen's head. "He's growing fast, Emily. This outfit is starting to get a bit tight on him."

"I noticed that when I dressed him this morning. But it's such a cute outfit I couldn't help but use it one more time." She paused in the middle of folding a shirt and looked down at her son with a loving smile. "Back to the job. You'll get another one, or will build your own company, but first you need to take care of that knee and do what your doctor tells you to do."

Lost in thought for a minute, "You've been too good to me, Em. And Declan. He should hate me after all I did to him as a kid. The torture and trauma." Talon bowed his head while holding onto Cailen with strong hands, a baby who was smiling and giggling and reaching out with his arms. Talon brought him to his chest and held him, gently patting his back.

"Talon, Declan loves you. He understands now. Yes, he worked very hard and is now a billionaire but just because your life took a different path doesn't mean you can't live the rest of it as a happy man. You are a very handsome man, Talon. You should be able to live a good life from now on." Putting all the folded clothing into a basket, "Here, give me Cailen."

Reaching down to retrieve her son, she smiled at hearing Cailen giggle when she held him close to her chest. "God, how I love this child. I swear to you Talon he will *never* suffer the pain that you and your brothers went through. But I also swear he will never be spoiled rotten. Your parents are gone now, God rest their souls, and only my mom is left to spoil him. She has been warned. None of this 75 gifts for Christmas. No child needs play stations, and he'll be monitored for the internet. He'll get lots of physical activity, like swimming and baseball…" Emily stopped talking as tears began to form in her eyes.

Talon gazed at Emily. She was so beautiful. Repressing his love for her was not easy, but necessary. It had to be channeled. If Declan hadn't stepped up to the plate and married her, he most certainly would have. And here they were, sitting in the kitchen of a magnificent mansion that had everything a man could want. He was forty-one years old. He needed to get his act together, and it was going to take a great deal of effort. Declan had given him a head's up on a different job opportunity that became available. It was one they were all sure would be right up his alley. Counseling. After what he had gone through, he would probably make an excellent counselor for alcoholics and womanizers. But for the moment he was happily busy with designing cabinets. He had managed to find a small shop to rent and had made some limited progress, but the few hours he spent in it every day were important to him. It wasn't a big space, but it suited his needs to build the cabinets, and had the nice option of expansion should he ever need it. What did surprise him was the growing demand for what he was making. Most of the home builders had begun checking out his designs, and it wouldn't be long before he'd have to hire some help. For reasons he didn't understand he loved working with wood, using his hands to create something beautiful and useful. It truly was a gift and he was getting more and more interested in using it for the rest of his life.

Picking up his cell phone he dialed his doctor's office and made an appointment. "OK, Em. I'll see the doctor tomorrow and ask for some therapy. Can I borrow one of the cars?"

"Talon," came a voice from the garage entryway, "You can always drive one of the cars anytime you need one. No need to ask."

"Hi, Declan," Talon replied, watching as Declan took Cailen from Emily's arms, holding him high in the air and smiling from ear to ear, seeing his beautiful son. Grabbing his little hand around his index finger he twirled him, listening to the beautiful chuckles that emitted from his son's face. Dropping Cailen to hold him cradled in his arms he turned, and gave Emily a short, but powerful kiss, complete with "Hi, gorgeous!"

Emily smiled. "Talon is going to go to the doctor to see about therapy for his knee."

"Good," observed Declan. "And listen, Talon. That job I told you about, the counseling one, is still available."

"I appreciate it, Declan. Truly. But I have to tell you I'm actually starting to thoroughly enjoy the little bit of money I'm making just building cabinets. I do a good job. It's surprising. I'll get this knee thing over with and then will be able to stand for more than a couple hours at a time.

"Define 'little bit of money,' Talon."

"I opened a bank account and before long I'll be able to apply for a credit card, I think."

"You're building these cabinets all by yourself?"

"For the moment. You know I found that small shop and it's getting so I have to go every day to keep up. Sold all my bathroom cabinets to a builder yesterday. He said it was some of the best work he'd ever seen."

Declan placed his hand on his brother's shoulder. "I had no idea. If things are going that well, and you love it, then that's the way to go. If you need legal advice, I have a wonderful attorney. Interesting!"

"Stop down and visit me one of these days."

"OK. I'd love to see it. Tomorrow afternoon?"

"I have a doctor appointment, but I'll be there in the afternoon."

"See you then?"

Nodding his head Talon stood and left the room. He had way too much to think about at this point in his life. There were too many different directions to go and he had no idea which one would be best. Picking up the laundry basket of folded clothing he headed up the stairs, a painful reminder that his knee was hurting badly going up steps. Stopping at the nursery he put the laundry basket down. Em and Declan had done a really good job on that room. Little animals wandering in and out of a forest scene, a crib, dresser, mom rocking chair and dad recliner. Totally perfect. Em's rocking chair was in a light green hue that blended in well with the forest colors, while Declan's walnut brown recliner was equally as excellent. Add a medium brown hardwood flooring that mimicked ground, and you'd swear you were really in the forest. Even the crib and dresser were a matching medium green color. Standing by one of the two large windows he could see the back yard in all its glory, beautiful grass, strong oak trees, situated well away from the home in case of weather-related problems. A small garden had been started in a corner, and he knew Em had plans to plant more herbs and veggies. She excelled at that kind of thing, apparently. One small area was dedicated to several bird feeders, all hanging from a well-trimmed willow tree. He needed to get a book on identifying birds. All he could see was a blue jay, a cardinal, and something yellow – smallish and beautiful flying to what he remembered being called thistle seed. He marveled at the size of the lot. It seemed to go on forever, with azaleas blooming and daffodils showing their yellow and white colors. He couldn't remember, in all his forty-one years, ever stopping to see anything having to do with nature. Just plain, old, everyday nature wasn't on his radar growing up. He'd had far more to worry about than roses and green grass for as long as he could remember.

With a sigh he walked back down the stairs and into the next wing and his rooms. Lying down on his bed he considered what his options were. OK, he thought. One – do nothing. But that would get old for all three of them. Two – Do therapy for his knee. Yeah, well. That was a given if he ever wanted to walk normally again. Three – check out the job offer Declan had mentioned, just to appease his brother. Four – Return to the drunk and addicted man he was before Declan rescued him. Five – get his butt in gear and go start making more cabinets. He was lucky at this point. He was his only help! But it was getting clearer that his work was getting good reviews. Five - Go back to Pennsylvania and see... That scared him to death. He grew up taking every woman he could get his hands on, single, married, divorced, widowed, he didn't have a preference. Loving them and then leaving them was the mantra of his days. He had no memory of who half of them were. And he knew if he went back to Pennsylvania there would be at least one more, if not ten, that would bring a child before him who called him "daddy." He already knew about two of them. It was entirely possible there were more. He had never used any protection and never asked if his latest conquest did either. He cringed at the very thought of that word, "daddy." It also struck him as odd that he had been *more* than willing to marry Emily and be a father to his brother's son. So much for a messed-up mind. And in the end, it was a lot of drama, but Declan had finally stepped up and married Emily. Deep in his heart he knew it was for the best, but GEEZE. He would have married Em in a minute. Declan had managed to overcome his demons. Now he needed to figure out what to do about his own. Choices. Far too many choices.

The ding of a bell stopped his wondering. Dinner was ready. Slowing making his way to the kitchen he knew, again, his knee wasn't going to fix itself.

"Oh, yum. Meatloaf," he sat down in his usual spot. Waiting for Declan to hold the chair for Em, and then seating himself into a chair, they began to eat. "Geeze, Em. This is really good," he commented, looking at her with appreciation. "We should let the chef have a day off more often!"

"Thanks, Talon." She couldn't help smiling. Emily had always been a good cook. She loved making meals for her family.

"How did your day go brother?" mumbled Talon between bites.

"Pretty much the same as always. More research and development. We're making advancements in the world of robotics for the physically challenged. And Em tells me if you don't watch that leg, you're going to be a nice candidate for one of our artificial limbs!"

Talon's head jerked to give Emily an evil eye. "Maybe not quite that bad, Talon, but you could well end up in pain and limping for the rest of your life. You aren't twenty anymore. You were lucky the original injuries healed. A knee replacement would be traumatic."

"Yeah, I get it," as he put his fork down. He guessed he needed the reminder. "I'll do the therapy after I see the doc tomorrow, *if* he thinks I need it."

"Good." Emily eyed him carefully. "Don't mess with this, Talon. You've walked back from hell this past year. Stay with it."

He could tell her eyes were ablaze with warning, and when Em stood her ground there was no hope for her target. Declan almost lost her forever with his idiot moves – at least

13

that was Talon's take on the whole scene. Declan had been stupid and Em had gotten pregnant. She was trying to find a new job in another state to quietly have Declan's baby and live her life as a single mom. She would have done it too. But then, he would have married her himself. He had told Declan that in no uncertain terms. Oh, the things we lose along the way, he thought. But, truth be told, he didn't even know she existed until his dad's funeral. And she only spoke to Declan at that time.

"OK, OK, I get it," he said. "I also hope to search for an apartment this coming weekend. There's a couple places at Meridian Obici, and maybe Beamons Mill, Autumn Ridge, and a couple of others. Just one bedroom. I need to give you guys your space and I need to find space of my own. I'm starting to do well with my cabinet business, so it shouldn't be a problem."

"I'll make it my priority to come see your business tomorrow," Declan said, looking at his brother with new eyes.

"I look forward to it," replied Talon.

As Talon left the kitchen to watch a game on his TV, Declan remained seated at the table and looking down, he began tapping his spoon gently on the napkin.

Emily could sense the mood change in her husband, noting the questioning in his eyes – concerned? Worried?

"Okay, tell me what you're thinking, Declan."

"Just wondering if he's healed enough, and I don't mean just physically, to head out on his own."

"I think," she said, as she began picking up dishes and setting them on the counter, "that the answer is yes. I've watched him. He hasn't had a drink since your mother died. I don't think he's a true alcoholic, just was a lost human being who had to gather women around him for any sense of love. I doubt he has a clue what real love is. But I will say that with your mom dying so suddenly after your dad, Talon took great pains to take care me. Especially… well…"

14

"Yes, when I brought another woman to Pennsylvania and missed Mom's funeral entirely."

"I never thought we would get past that, Declan."

"Well it sure shocked me into some serious thinking. I wonder if you'll ever know how much I love you." Staring up at her, standing in front of him, apron on, hands gathering dishes, seeing her with Cailen. His heart was bursting. Yet it was Talon who had given him that last *very* solid kick in the butt to go after her. Thank God.

"I just hope he finds someone to love and build a family with," she said.

"He was sure gaining on that thought with you, Emily."

"Yes, I know, Declan. I was always aware of his feelings for me once we started his therapy. Most was typical transference, and he'll get over it"

"Would you have married him if I hadn't followed you?"

"A good question, my dear husband." Glancing at her hands, folded in front of her apron, she cocked her head, deeply in thought. "I have to put myself back in that place. You must understand that. You had hurt me *so* deeply in the month preceding. Beyond hurt. There I sat, having literally been tossed out once in a dripping bathing suit. It was the last twist of the knife. So…" Looking straight at Declan and locking eyes with him, "Yes, I would have married Talon to give the baby a Seaton last name."

Declan sighed, but then smiled. "Thank you for your honesty, Emily. I just thank God I got there in time to make you my wife."

"I think all Talon needs to do is find a beautiful woman to love and he'll be the best brother-in-law ever. So yes, I think he's ready to have his own place, at the ripe old age of 41!"

Leaning down she kissed him on his forehead. "You can now take the trash out."

He did as he was told.

Chapter 2

Talon breezed out of the doctor's office with four pieces of paper in his hands. Each one had a different exercise for him to do for half an hour, twice a day, to strengthen his knee. If that didn't work after a month then he'd have to make room for some real physical therapy.

Things were beginning to look up. It wasn't that all his problems and issues had vanished. He had a long way to go but hoped to be able to do it without any more psychological counseling. He knew, deep down, that he would never be able to do a counseling job. Despite his recovery from the booze, some minor drugs that he had managed to keep Em and Declan from knowing about, and just general deprivation, along with some serious malnutrition, he didn't think he would be able to sit across the desk from someone equally as damaged and be able to handle their stories. Instinctively he knew it would be all too easy to be drawn back into that life. It was a daily struggle to remain stable as it was, and it required some heavy-duty willpower to avoid temptations on some of the tougher days. On those days he tried to zero in on Emily and Cailen, watching them move and work and play. It grounded him and made him wish for the same kind of life for himself. Maybe he'd get lucky, before he died of old age, and would find some lovely woman to marry.

Opening his shop, he walked into one of the most wonderful smells on earth. Wood shavings. The only thing that smelled better was, maybe, a new car, and sadly, Emily. The scent of her hair and body lotions kept him on his toes. It wasn't easy reminding himself of how close he had been to becoming her husband. Well, at least in his own mind.

Letting out a gigantic breath he picked up a piece of wood and headed over to the table saw. With his ear and eye protection in place he turned the machine on and began cutting the pieces for the next cabinet. As the saw whirled down to a stop, he turned to see Declan standing in the doorway. "Come on in, Declan. I apologize for the wood dust that is getting on that beautiful suit!"

"This is amazing, Talon. I'm not kidding. I had no idea you were this prolific!" Looking around he saw several cabinets in the 'finished' category, and more in various stages of completion. Walking up to examine one of them, "These are *really* nice."

Talon walked over and fingered the wood. "The finished ones are going to be picked up later today. The ones in progress need to be ready in two days. It's nice to know they are selling, anyway."

"Makes me want to redo the house," said Declan. "Nice wood, silent drawers. Good work!" Glancing around the room, "I must say you have certainly gotten the best equipment for what you are doing."

"Yeah. I'm going to have to hire help pretty soon. Like maybe this week. I can't keep up with the paperwork, and now the orders are starting to back up."

"It appears like you have enough equipment to do the job right now. Co-signing that small loan for you was a good bet. Not that I had any doubts."

"Yes, you did. I could tell you were having a hard time figuring out how I could make anything out of wood, let alone cabinets. Especially since I had spent most of my life going from woman to woman and drinking my day away."

"It was a gut move, that's true, Talon. But you were making progress and that needed to be rewarded. Your promise to do a good job made me want to help you with a good start. You proved you were determined, so I wanted to do something to show I trusted your judgement. Regardless of our past growing up, Talon, you are my brother."

Talon was silent. Picking up a brush he started to dust some of the wood shavings off the counter. "Sorry, brother, but even with a vacuum system there's no way to catch all the flying wood when you saw."

"I'm guessing the contractor or builder selects the counter tops when these are installed?"

"Yes, for the most part. If it's just a single vanity type cabinet for a small bathroom then I can often work with the owner to put the countertop on, but if it's a complete kitchen or custom bathroom with double sinks and all then the countertops have to be custom made after the cabinets are installed."

"Where on earth did you learn all this?"

"I used to do some work in construction when I needed a few bucks. A furniture maker in Defiance liked my work and I would work with him occasionally. When I was, shall we say, soberer. He's really, really good. Taught me a lot about dove joints and finishing. Said I was a natural. Maybe I am. I can pretty much make most anything. I'd like to get into furniture but need to get some help in here first. Especially someone to keep the books and paperwork straight."

"Can I give you some advice?"

"Sure."

"For the paperwork! Hire an older woman, married, with grown children, and *pay her well.* Your business depends on it."

"Why?"

"Because you are one hell of a good-looking guy, Talon. You have somehow maintained your rugged features with gray eyes, and a tight, firm body. The slightly salt-and-pepper hair only adds to the image. On any dance floor in town you would have them lined up to dance with you. Just to get their bare hands on you. I know I'm talking to the choir, but you should be able to figure it out for yourself, since you never, in all your years, had any problem attracting the ladies." Eyeing his brother, he realized that Talon had no clue how good looking he really was. "And if they knew who your brother really was, you wouldn't be able to get rid of them."

"You're kidding."

"I guarantee you I'm not. Think what will happen if you bring in some 21-year-old college graduate with no experience. Knowing you, she'd be a stunner. Her body would be honed. She'd start wearing low cut and see-through blouses. Her skirts would get shorter and shorter while your eyes would get bigger and bigger, Talon. She'd bat her eye lashes and lick her lips and set her sights. I'd give it a month before you're taking her to your bed. Probably much less. Then what?"

"OK. I see that happening for sure."

"Exactly. Good. Now, hire an older woman, or man, and their loyalty will be immediate. Even if you hire part-time or let them work from home. That paperwork, along with the ongoing skill level of your work, is all it will take to get a booming business going. You said you've already established a good relationship with several of the construction companies. Your networking is excellent. In five years, you'll have one hundred workers turning out the best furniture money can buy, and trust me, despite the small town you are now living in there *is* money all around you. Just think of the

Armada Hoffler Towers or King's Grant in Virginia Beach. Ghent in Norfolk, to name a few."

Paying attention wasn't one of Talon's strong suits, unless, of course, he was intent on landing a woman for the night, but he had to admit that Declan had some outstanding advice for him. Declan was absolutely right. He would have lasted, perhaps a week, before getting fixated on some young woman doing the paperwork. And when the relationship ended badly who knew what revenge she might take. Good thinking, Declan! He certainly would never have hired a plain-Jane for the job, so he was setting himself up for a complete failure if he didn't start thinking with his head instead of his emotions.

"I see exactly what you mean, Declan. Old habits die hard. I'd have done the wrong thing for sure, just as you described it. Older, competent, experienced. Yes. Thanks."

"You're welcome. By the way, what about the knee and therapy?"

"Doc gave me some exercises to do twice a day and if I do what I'm supposed to do then I should be fine without formal therapy."

"Emily will be glad to hear that, Talon. She really cares about you, despite her reticence."

"I realize that. It's hard, Declan."

"Talon, I really understand. I haven't said anything because it pains me to know how badly I acted after you came down from Pennsylvania. Deep down I knew I loved her, but I couldn't admit it. I had made such a mess of the one time I made love to her. I was so embarrassed by it all. I just couldn't face her. When you ruined your knee, it seemed like a gift from the gods. Bring you down and have her do your therapy. That way I could keep seeing her. Keep up with what she was doing."

Talon had taken a seat on one of the stools. Wiping another one off, and bringing it closer to him, he offered it to Declan, who immediately sat down. Pausing, Declan looked down at his hands, carefully folded on his lap. "It backfired on me. I could tell," he was still looking at his hands, which hadn't moved at all, "that you were falling for her. I couldn't be sure if she was returning that emotion, but it was clear you were having a problem with it."

"Yeah, I know," whispered Talon, shifting on the stool as he ran his fingers through his hair. "I'm sorry about that, Declan."

"There's nothing to be sorry for, Talon. I put both of you into that situation. I was trying to figure out if it was for real, or just one of those patient-doctor kind of love things. When I saw the two of you together, I went crazy. Angry. Over the top. Throwing paychecks, yelling hurtful words. *GOD!*" Declan raised his hands and slapped them back down again on his thighs. "I think back and am stunned at my behavior. Jealous to the nth degree. Livid with jealousy. Then when you told me about the baby I came as close to losing it as I ever could."

Hearing the pain in his brother's voice, Talon could tell that it was extremely difficult for Declan to be verbalizing those thoughts and emotions. "Declan, look at me."

When Declan looked up, "I would have married her, you know."

"Oh, I know. I finally knew the rest of my life depended on my decision that day. You gave me thirty minutes to go after her, or you would go. That was not only the most agonizing day of my life but the most pleasing in the end. I could almost hear your heart breaking when I called to ask you to be my Best Man. I am so sorry I put you in that position, Talon. You have no idea"

"I have an idea, for sure. Yes. Seeing her every day is still hard. Harder on some days than others, but I need to find my own place to live or I'll never move on from that day. It haunts me. I would *never* do anything to hurt either you or Em, and I think you know that. But my heart hurts sometimes when I look at her, and I know it will just take time. It will happen. I will find someone to love and hopefully settle down, and peace will follow." Locking eyes with his brother, "Just don't you *ever* forget how lucky you are, Declan."

Standing up Declan moved the two steps to hug his brother. "You have no idea how happy I am to have you, and our other two brothers, back in my life."

"I'm just thankful you forgave me for all the harm I did to you as a child."

"I like to think it made us both stronger in the end, Talon."

Curling his lips up a bit, in a smile, "That's for sure. We survived."

"What will your next step be, then?"

Talon thought for a second. "If you have any recommendations for a secretary/accountant, I'd love to interview them. Or, I can put an ad in the newspaper. I can also ask my customers if they have any recommendations. Heaven knows the sooner I get someone in here, the better it will be. I also want to hire at least two more carpenters. I need someone who is qualified in staining and painting, and another one for construction. I would like to move into furniture before too long, as well."

"I'll check with Millie, my own accountant, and see if she has any friends who could use a job like this."

Smiling, Talon couldn't help but take the brush to Declan's suit coat. "You do know that Em is going to kill you when you walk into her spotless home with all this dust on this gorgeous, expensive suit, right?"

"Her home?" Declan laughed. "Oh, how right you are, Talon!"

Chapter 3

True to his word Talon spent the entire next weekend searching for a place to live. Expensive was the word he used for everything he toured, even one-bedroom apartments. He was making good money and easily paying off the loan that Declan had co-signed, but both Declan and Talon knew he had to move. Both figured that Em really didn't know how much hurt was still in his heart. It was good to move out before something happened. He would never do anything to hurt either Em or Declan, but he dreaded that something simple would send him back to the booze. Seeing her hold Cailen made him think about how nice life could be if he had his own family. That nugget of thought was stuck in his mind, now, and he needed to break out of his shell and figure out some way to lead his own life. Unfortunately, each place he visited had something he didn't like about it. Third floor. One bedroom (he had decided he wanted two). Crummy view. Not up to his standards of construction. Bad location for what he needed. It was discouraging, but he had to keep up the pace.

He finally settled on an apartment in Hampton Roads Crossing, just a few miles from where Declan lived. Completely empty and a first-floor location, to keep it easy on his knee, it was available immediately. All repair work and repainting had already been done, new carpet, and completely clean. It was twenty miles from his workspace, which he had set up in a converted old peanut factory in downtown Suffolk, but traffic wasn't bad as a rule. Arriving back at Declan's for Sunday dinner he felt like he might finally become an adult, at the ripe old age of 41.

As he sat down at the table, napkin in his lap, and fork poised above the beautiful piece of chicken on his plate, "Well, you two, I finally found a place to live, so I'll be moving out next weekend."

"WOW," expressed Emily. "That's a fast one."

"Yup. Moving on. But not too far. Just about 3 miles to the apartments at Hampton Roads Crossing."

"Good for you, Talon." Declan was obviously impressed with what his brother had done. "One step at a time, and you're sure doing just that. Now a good business going, a new apartment… sounds like things are falling into place."

All three of them continued to eat, and between bites, Talon looked at his brother, "Declan, I'm going to start checking out applicants for that accountant tomorrow. So, if Millie knows anyone like you were describing, have her give me a call. I'll set up an appointment."

Emily looked at Talon, and it didn't escape her notice that he wasn't looking at her. She would deal with that later. There was an obvious elephant in the room, but none of them wanted to address it. Even though they had spoken individually – Emily to Talon, (but obliquely), Talon to

Declan, Declan to Emily – for some unknown reason they couldn't seem to be comfortable enough to talk about it between the three of them. There had been so much pain and hurt involved in the therapy help that Emily had provided that it really was hard to heal the scars that still remained.

No sooner had Talon excused himself from dinner than Emily cleared her throat. "Ahem, ah, Declan, what was that all about?"

"What was what all about?"

"Give me a break, will you? Talon. An accountant. Someone you were 'describing' (she made air quotes) to him."

Declan screws his lips up to the side and wiped his hands off on the napkin in his lap. "Well, he's needs paperwork help and it would be best if he had someone who could answer the phones at the same time. I just advised him against hiring some sweet young thing who would want to get him undressed as fast as she could manage it."

"I can't say that's anything other than very good advice." Standing, she began to clear the table of dishes.

"Yeah." Declan wiped his mouth, "I told him maybe Millie might have a friend who was older, more mature, married, stable – you get the drill – who would be better at that kind of job. What I didn't tell him as she would make an excellent 'mother' figure at the same time. Keep him in line. Monitor what he does."

"Are you saying you want a spy in his office?" She gave him a horrified gasp.

"No. Not at all," he winced. "It just might be a normal thing for her to do, especially if she had grown children of her own. I know Talon isn't twenty, and that might make a difference, but it's worth a shot to have a nice, matronly, motherly person who might hopefully take over that role naturally." He smiled. "Yeah. I'm gonna mention that to Millie."

"I can understand where you're coming from," Em admitted. "The last thing we want is to have him set himself up in a situation that might make him regress, but we need to keep from interfering or being overprotective. He has to finish finding his way by himself, Declan. Just let him know we're always here if something happens that makes him nervous."

He studied her as she leaned down to finish loading the dishwasher. For the rest of his life he would owe his happiness to the brother that had tortured him as a child. He would spend the rest of his life doing whatever was necessary to help Talon. He thought what it would have been like to come home each night and not have Em and Cailen there. They were his life. He adored them, and it was Talon that had made it all happen.

Returning to his room Talon realized he didn't have all that much packing to do. What was going to be fun was getting at least a bed and chair and kitchen table to start his new life in his own apartment. With a couple of drawers open and his suitcase on his bed, he turned to see Declan standing in the doorway.

"Not a whole lot to move, I gather," observed Declan.

Talon laughed. "I'll manage. I supposed I can crash here until I at least get a bed and chair into my apartment."

"Not to worry. I have a ton of older furniture, still in excellent shape, in a storage unit not far from here. Seems my little wife has done a bit of upgrading." He smiled. "If you want to go over there early tomorrow with me you can pick out what you want, and I'll have it delivered. Just give me the key to your place."

"That's incredible. I really appreciate it."

"If you empty the place out, I can have one less thing on my mind! In a way I'm surprised you didn't notice the change in furniture in most of the rooms."

"I'm not the observant type. At least I wasn't. Getting better now that my head is straight, but even at that, being attentive at what I'm sitting in hasn't usually made an impression on me," Talon was smiling from ear to ear. "I only paid attention to women's bodies – what I could do to them.

What they could do for me. Hmm." Snapping his attention back to Declan, "What time tomorrow morning?"

"How about six?"

"Sounds good, Declan. Thanks again."

Talon was thrilled. That left him with only food, some utensils to cook and eat with, a few dishes. He could pick all that up tomorrow between the grocery store and the Dollar Tree. He didn't need fancy, just utilitarian, so dishes and forks from Dollar Tree would do just fine. His mental list started to expand. There was already a washer and dryer and fridge in the new place. But that meant he needed soap. Soap for the washer and the dishwasher. Shower curtain. Add shower curtain. The waffle blinds already there would do fine. Broom. Mop. Vac. Well, one thing at a time, then. As needed!

"Holy Cow!" exclaimed Talon. "You weren't kidding. Em has totally taken over the house décor! I had no idea you were talking about a whole house full of furniture in the largest storage container in the county."

"Well, we emptied out one of the guest rooms to make it a nursery. So that gives you a queen size bed and two dressers. Then she wanted different chairs in the entertainment room, so you can have those. Some lamps and stuff she didn't particularly like. Top it off with a rather nice kitchen table and chairs and you should be set for a while. So – are you going to clean me out here?"

"I certainly will. This is amazing. And I see more than one bed so I can even grab enough stuff for a guest room. Saving us both big bucks, and I can use it all. And I *like* the lamps."

"I have no idea what all is in here. She had it picked up and stored, and now it's a good thing she did, I guess."

"No kidding. When my funds get a bit thicker, I'll pay you for it all."

"No, you won't. You're going to be saving me storage fees, so it's a win-win."

"I have never owned anything in my whole life, Declan. The mattresses I would sleep on were all grabbed from dump sites. Never owned a chair or television. Bathroom was in the woods, and I'm here to tell you that hurts in the middle of winter. I don't know what to say, except I'll do everything I can to make you proud."

Declan reached up and put his arm around Talon's shoulders. "You're doing just fine in that regard, Talon. Can you meet a truck during your lunch hour to help them put the big things into the right room?"

"Done."

"OK, I'm going to go on in to work. You go ahead and keep using that car until you find time to get one you want. I don't need four cars."

"Not to mention the limo, huh?"

"No kidding. And, if you want, heck… I'll even sell you the one you are driving. Like I said… life tends to change when one gets married." He chuckled. "Priorities," he smacked his lips.

"Might just do that too, Declan. I'm going to run back to the house and pick up my luggage. That should give the housekeeper time to clean it out and turn it back into a nice guest room!"

Driving back toward Declan's home he couldn't help but realize how very blessed he was. He knew there was no way he could ever pay back all that Declan had given him, so he was just going to be the best brother ever. Pulling into the garage, he thought again about the car. Nice car. Two years old. Walking around it…yes, very nice car… totally worth seeing if Declan was serious about selling it to him. Hmm – his thoughts jumped – toilet paper, shower soap, towels – now that would have been cute, emerging from the shower with nothing to use to dry off. He wondered how long it would take to dry if you were dripping wet.

Entering the kitchen Emily was sitting at the table. "Hi, Em! Where's Cailen? I'll just pick up my suitcase and be out of your hair."

"Talon, please sit down."

Well, thought Talon, that didn't sound good. "OK, what's up?"

"First, I'm pleased to see you doing so well, and so quickly. It means more than you know to both Declan and me. Second," she paused to fold her hands and check out her fingernails, then lifted her eyes back up, "I understand what goes on in your heart, Talon. I know you were ready to ask me to marry you to give Declan's child a Seaton last name. And you loved me. You still do. I know about the thirty-minute warning, and how it must have hurt you to know that Declan suddenly realized he was in love with me and asked me to marry him. I just," she paused a second time to look directly into his eyes, "I just want you to know that you'll always be more than a brother-in-law to me. You are so special, Talon, and you'll find a wonderful woman to spend the rest of your life with. I just know it."

Standing, Talon walked over to her and lifted her chin as he placed a tender kiss on her cheek. "Thanks, Em. It is what it is. You both know there's nothing I wouldn't do for you guys."

"I just want it to all be out in the open, Talon. All three of us know the dynamics of those last few days, and there isn't a single thing to be ashamed of. The only man I've ever loved is Declan, from the age of four. A few dates here and there but Declan never left my mind. I didn't think I'd ever see him again to be honest. Figured I'd just end up a little old lady, living alone, with three cats and a dog. But life snuck up on all of us. I thank God it all came together in the end."

"It's no secret," he gave Em a toothy grin, "that I would have married you. A bit hard to admit, maybe, but you belong with Declan. I always realized that. He was just being such an idiot. He loved you but his ego was getting in the way. So," he dusted off his hands," I took care of that little problem. We're fine, Em. And always will be."

Slowly walking upstairs, he felt like his heart had dropped to his stomach, but he was sure this was the right thing to do. He badly needed to get his focus shifted to taking control of his own life and not needing any more handouts. His entire life had been nothing but hand-me-downs and taking things people would give him, whether out of pity or necessity he had no clue. But now his business was growing rapidly, and he had to start doing some serious planning to get it growing the way he needed it to grow. He would be interviewing applicants for an accountant. With luck someone would call today, just from word of mouth, and the quick ad he had placed on the internet.

He no sooner opened the door to his office than he heard his phone ringing. One woman was calling about the job, so he told her to come on over. Apparently, she had called from a block away as she was immediately opening the door to his shop. And it wasn't just her. She had her daughter with her. Yes. A stunner of a daughter. A stunner dressed inappropriately in a tight dress that was way too short, and breasts just a quarter inch shy of nipple exposure.

"Are you Talon?" the mother cooed. "I hope you don't mind my daughter being with me, as we saw your ad and your picture, and I would love to work for you."

Holy Crap, he thought. The daughter was already giving him the eye, complete with licking her lips, and doing her best to get close to him. Declan had certainly been on target with that description. He had to bite his tongue to keep from laughing. Instead, he kept moving backwards, "Did you bring a resume of past jobs?"

"Not with me. This was so sudden. But I worked for the peanut processing company that was in this area. They closed shop, so I was out of a job."

Talon kept circling as daughter kept maneuvering to get close to him. "Well, tell you what. Send me the resume in the mail and I'll get back to you for an interview. I have several interviews today," he lied, "so I won't be making any decisions until later this week."

"Can we stay and watch you work?" meowed the daughter, still trying to get close to him.

"Absolutely not. Insurance forbids it. I can't do anything while you are in here. So, I do have other appointments arriving shortly," he lied again, "so I will let you know."

Turning to walk to the door to open it for them, daughter brushed into him, with a sweet smile, again licking her lower lip. Slipping her phone number into his hand, she slinked out the door. He couldn't wait to close it. Placing his back against the closed door he wiped the sweat off his brow and looked back out to be sure they were gone. Tossing the piece of paper into the trash he was astonished at what he had just gone through. Even with all the women he chased in Defiance, not a single one of them was that aggressive. They all loved him. Worse, they all wanted him – as a husband! And as soon as he got that message, he dropped them and moved on. He hoped he hadn't been cruel, but he was mostly drunk or high and could not be considered even remotely sane. He wasn't living a hermit's life, but he was a derelict for over thirty years. For sure. A derelict. He had a lot to come back from and he intended to do it.

His next three interviews during the week went well, and all had come prepared. Meeting Declan for lunch he went over the list with him.

"Well, the first one is the most amazing and never sent a resume. She actually brought her daughter, who was dressed more like a harlot than a lady. Funny that the mother never did send in a resume." He told Declan about the exit door shenanigans!

Declan couldn't help but laugh. "Your past just bumped into you and you turned your back on it. I love it. Well done, Talon."

"Then," Talon grabbed another piece of paper, "Number 2. She was OK, qualified, but a bit too young. Maybe 45. Divorced, one grown daughter. Pretty. Too tempting." More paper shuffling, "Number 3 was fine age-wise and all, but she didn't have a whole lot of recent experience. So that's where I am right now. I have one more interview this afternoon. I really need to get someone to do all this stuff. I also have my eye on a couple of Amish gentlemen I just heard about. They do a lot of furniture but lost their lease and no longer work. They might like to work for me."

"You've been on fire, Talon. And let me check with Millie again. She thought she might have a line on someone she trusted who was either retired or laid-off." Picking up his cell phone he punched in his 'favorites' screen and tapped the button. "Millie, thought I'd check on the possible lead you might have for an accountant for Talon... OK... Yes... Excellent. I'll tell him. Hold on for a minute..." Turning to Talon, "Are you free this afternoon, before or after your other interview?" Talon nodded yes. "My interview is at 2 P.M., and should be over by 2:30, so any time before or after."

"Millie, can she make it at 3 P.M? Perfect. Thanks. I'll be back in the office soon."

"OK, Anna will be in to see you at 3. According to Millie she was laid-off from her job at one of the peanut companies. She's highly qualified, keeps confidences, is 62 years old, two children grown, and a husband who loves her."

"Like grabbing the gold ring on the merry-go-round!"

"Keep me posted. I need to get back to work."

Chapter 4

Finally, it had come together. Anna was indeed perfect for the job as accountant and paper pusher. He knew he'd have to hire someone else to do the ordering and all that, but for the moment Anna was completely competent to do it all. The best part - she was simply a very nice lady!

The bonus for him was hiring the two Amish men to help him in the shop. Both were so incredibly talented he knew immediately that they would fit into his business. Talon couldn't believe his good luck. It had been so empowering to realize he had a growing and stable business, a nice new apartment, completely furnished for free, and the knowledge that he was finally on the right track. Now to become involved in some kind of community endeavor. He didn't want anything to do with booze or drugs. He never wanted to even *think* about either of those again. He did want to become part of the larger picture though, and community service was a good way to start. Declan could guide him, and some of the contractors he was getting to know would have an idea or two of where he could be of use to the local area.

The only 'hiccup' in his current life was Emily, and he knew, deep down, that it would pass. It simply had to. As Declan had said, it was probably more a therapist/patient love, which escalated when he had discovered her pregnancy during one of their therapy sessions. He shivered. That really was a horrible couple of weeks.

Before Talon knew it, Spring had arrived. His company had been moving along at a rapid pace. He now did the work for two different home construction companies and was keeping up with the work so far. His talented Amish craftsmen were just amazing, and he was an eager student to two gentlemen who had been making furniture since they were children. Learning different ways to cut and put furniture together was fascinating. There was more than one way to do the job. They were worth their weight in gold. Not only was he grateful to have them but they were equally as grateful to have a job. They didn't need any direction or instruction. Truth be known the opposite was true. It was perfect.

Called into the office, Anna advised him that one of the contractor's site supervisors was there to see if a cabinet order could be delivered early.

Wiping the dust off his hands, and lightly brushing his clothing (Anna was not appreciative of saw dust all over her desk), he opened the door to the office.

And he stood there like a statue.

She took his breath away. Just one look as he walked in the door and he was stunned.

"Talon, this is one of Al's site supervisors, Mariah Rogers."

Each held out a hand to shake, and Talon nearly jumped at the spark he felt. Quickly gathering his thoughts, "What can I do for you Mariah?" Good grief, was that a show of nervousness? He was shaking a bit. Did she notice? Did Anna notice? Anna didn't miss much.

"Al and I were wondering if there was any way the cabinets for section 'B' could be delivered early?"

"Let me check. I'll be right back."

Going back into the shop he blew out a long, deep breath, and leaned his back against the wall, out of sight for a second. Holy cow! He needed to check and see if there were any rings on her fingers. He was so shocked at her beautiful, porcelain face, long brunette hair, incredible figure and narcotic inducing smile that he could barely control himself. Shuffling his feet to make sure he was grounded, "Aaron," he called out. "Where are we at on the section 'B' cabinets for Devon construction?"

"Finishing up on the last one, Talon. Will be ready tomorrow."

"Thanks. Excellent." Waved Talon, as he returned to the office.

"We can deliver tomorrow. Last one is being worked on now." It was all he could do to take his eyes off her, and he finally remembered to look at her hands. *No rings.* Good sign.

"Tomorrow would be outstanding. Al will be thrilled. Perhaps I'll see you there," she said with a shy smile.

"Perhaps you will, Mariah. Thanks for stopping by."

"Bye," was all she said, smiling slightly as she turned to walk away, and raising her right hand to her waist in a small wave. As she slowly closed the door behind her Talon found his feet nailed to the floor, watching every move, right to the very small 'click' as the door was secured. Turning his head to peer through the window, he heard a small, soft giggle behind him. He turned to look at Anna.

"What?"

"Oh, Talon. You are so toast!"

His bright, gray eyes looked at her. "No kidding," was all he could think to say.

Would tomorrow *never come*?

Mariah held her breath as she listened to the door closing behind her. Al had told her that this new cabinet subcontractor was good looking, but that didn't come close to what Mariah had seen walk into the office. He seemed to be rather shy, but he had definitely noticed her. She was sure of that when she saw the stunned look in his eye.

She was 30 years old and not one to find any satisfaction in dating. Quite the opposite, in fact. She had come to the conclusion that most men were juveniles, and better left to their own devices. She didn't have any problems living alone or being alone. She had one or two friends, but they weren't close, mostly because they had married and were now mothers. But she saw them a couple times a year. Her brother lived in Richmond with his wife and child, and she tried to visit them as time allowed. These days, however, Al kept her so busy with the supervisor job at a construction site she didn't have time to think much about dating *or* visiting. Even her mom had given up asking her about possible boyfriends. She loved her mom and wished she would move back down to Virginia now that her dad had died. She made it a point to try to call her more often and would even find a way to visit her for a couple days every three or four months. That usually meant flying to Cleveland to do it, since it was a ten-hour drive that could eat up two days just in travel.

This was the first moment in many, many years that she even gave thought to dating. She couldn't get the face of that incredibly handsome Talon out of her mind. Tomorrow could be an interesting day. All she could do was hope that what she had felt when she saw Talon would be reciprocated by his appearing at the delivery site with those cabinets. That would tell her volumes.

"Declan," he said over his iPhone, "Are you free for lunch?"

"I can do that. Local to my office though."

"How about the deli on the next block?"

"Noon OK?"

"Noon it is."

Talon was already seated in a booth when Declan entered. Quickly ordering a Reuben sandwich, to match Talon's order, "What's up, brother?"

"I just need a bit of advice. I'm still learning some of this kind of thing. I'm a bit scared I'll do the wrong thing"

"Shoot!"

Describing the events that had just taken place in his office, "Do you think it's okay if I ask her out for a date? I mean, she's a site supervisor to Al, who owns Devon Construction, and they get all their cabinets from me. I don't want to cross any lines."

Standing to remove his suit coat, and reseating himself as he straightened his tie, Declan put his hands together and looked at his brother. "I think, just from what I can see of you, that you are toast."

"Funny, that's exactly what Anna said when Mariah closed the door upon leaving."

"And…"

"My heart went to my toes when I saw her. I know it's an old line, but really, Declan, she just took my breath away. She's not wearing any rings. Appears to be in her early to mid-thirties. I don't want to start anything that can't be finished."

"Is Al married?"

"Yes, wife and 4 kids no less."

"You said her last name was Rogers. And Al's last name is Rogers. Any relationship?"

"Oh! My thinking hadn't gotten that far. Maybe he's her dad?

"Or brother. Or Uncle. Or cousin."

"I'll ask her if I decide to see if she's interested."

I see no problem. So, if you see her tomorrow then ask her out to dinner or ask for her phone number or something like that. Then see how she responds. You'll have your answer then."

"OK. I'll try it. Thanks. How are Em and Cailen doing?"

"Just fine. I swear, Cailen grows another inch every day. He's going to be one big guy, I think. Emily has started reading books to him already. Says he can't start learning too soon! She's amazing."

"Both of you are amazing."

Talon had been so intense in his questioning that he'd forgotten to eat. But Declan had to get back to work so Talon shook his hand and told him to go ahead. He would stay and eat his lunch. He watched as his brother picked up his empty plate and cup and properly disposed of them. Two bites into his Reuben he couldn't help but think about Mariah. But gosh, she was beautiful. He couldn't get her out of his mind. He had spent the past year fighting to get his internal compass back to true north, and now he had found a woman that eclipsed his thoughts of Em. Fascinating. Em had said he would find the perfect woman. Gosh, he prayed she was right about what might happen with Mariah. Still, he had to be on his guard. As beautiful and soft as Mariah seemed to be it was totally possible she was an egotistical witch once you got to know her. Baby steps, Talon, baby steps!

That night he tossed and turned. It was unusual for him to be so restless. He thought of, probably, a thousand ways to ask her out and wasn't happy with any of them. Dozing off for about an hour he was rudely awakened by his alarm clock. Even a hot shower didn't diminish his thoughts, and now he was adding a bit of fear to the problem. Shaving carefully and using his best aftershave lotion he dressed in some of his 'better' work clothing. Nothing spectacular. Just a relatively new pair of jeans and a much nicer polo shirt. He didn't doubt that Anna would catch the change in his attire. Like he already had figured out, she never missed a thing.

Arriving at work he was pleased to see Jacob and Aaron already loading the van. Smartest thing he had done was buy that oversized van to transport cabinets. It would hold six. He was only transporting five. Driving slowly to keep them from shuffling around he arrived at Section B right on schedule and standing before him… he was filled with her beauty while sensing his anxiety level increasing… *just get out of the van, Talon. She doesn't bite. Just be natural. Ask her where she wants the cabinets to be taken. Keep it simple. Slow down heart rate.* This was all so totally new to him he was at a loss as to how to proceed. Women had always chased *him*. This was a whole new way of life!

"Hi, Mariah! Where would you like us to take the cabinets?" He was shaking but her bright, cheery smile kept him grounded.

He watched, almost playing the action in slow motion, as Mariah lifted her arm and pointed to a location. She walked toward him and extended her hand. Taking it, he froze for a second, but her "Talon, how nice to see you again," brought his focus back to earth, and he directed Aaron and Jacob to the correct site.

"Let's follow them and I'll be able to tell them the exact place to set them down. Three are for the kitchen and one each for bathrooms."

Still holding his hand, she turned and began walking into the house. "This is just so amazing, Talon. You have no idea how grateful we are to have this done early. We have a buyer with an immediate need for it, so we are pulling out all the stops to get it finished by the middle of next week. He's out today selecting cabinet tops, which is really the only thing left to finish. He can deal with some particle board for countertops until the Corian he selects is delivered in another two to three weeks."

"I'm glad we could be of service, Mariah." Suddenly feeling he couldn't ask her out to her face, "let me know if we can help in any other way." *Oh, Talon,* he thought. *You squirming, little yellow-back. Six months ago, you were hauling women into your shed by their hair! Now you can't even speak two sentences in correct order!*

"Actually," Mariah said, "I was wondering if you'd like to join me for lunch? I had to get here early so haven't had time to even get a cup of coffee."

"I haven't had coffee yet either," smiled Talon. "I'd love to have lunch with you." *Pretty much every day!*

Sending the crew back with the van, Talon joined Mariah in her car.

"Are you from this area?" Talon ventured to ask.

"Born and raised. How about you?"

"A little town called Defiance, in Pennsylvania. Near Bedford."

"Ah, I'm familiar with the area. I've driven through there on my way to Cleveland. Both my parents were from Cleveland originally."

"How did you come about working for Al?"

"Al is my uncle. He and my dad started this business, after Dad got out of the Navy, and Al kept it going after my dad died."

"I'm sorry. I just lost both my mom and dad, so I know…"

He stopped. What did he know? His mother and father had abused him horribly. In turn he had abused Declan. If not for the families of his friends, he would have starved to death. No, he couldn't empathize with the loss of her dad. He had no feelings for either of his parents.

Reaching over and touching his hand, Mariah grasped it for a moment, sending Talon's heart racing, just as they were turning into the parking lot of a small diner. "I love this place. Great food, good prices. It's my little secret hiding place. They open at 11 for lunch and stay open until 2 A.M., so it's a nice diversion!"

"Shamrock Pub!" Sounds interesting. He watched as she pulled into the parking lot behind the pub.

Getting out of the car he quickly followed her, getting to the door just a split second before she did. Opening it, she turned and grinned, "Thank you," she whispered. Placing his hand on her back as they entered felt so, so, right. He liked the feeling, and even better she didn't seem to be rejecting it. Walking up a small stairway, he noticed a sign that said to seat themselves, and it was clear that it was a tiny place, but homey and comfortable. Toward the back he noted a small raised area where a band could play and just enough room for a few people to dance. He had no doubt that lunch and dinner were probably filled to the brim with patrons. The paneling was a dark wood, and there were several tables around the small room.

Opening menus, he glanced across at her, "What's good? What do you recommend? This is some amazing menu. They seem to serve just about everything."

Following her suggestions, they were served with hamburgers, fries and coffee. As much as both would have loved a beer, Talon declined for obvious reasons, although he said it was because he had to go back to work with power tools. Both dove into their food, hungry. After a few bites, "So you just started working for your dad and uncle after college?"

"Yes, I have a business degree, so they figured I'd be useful," she said laughing. "They thought they conned me, but I've loved every single minute of it. I actually started out as a gofer but did so well at managing all that – rather like a juggler, that they turned me into a receptionist. From there I started going out to make sure everything was on site when a supervisor was sick or on vacation. Did such a good job they gave it to me! And I love it."

"I'm guessing it's a bit unusual to have a woman supervising an entire build. Do the guys give you a lot of trouble… the workers?"

"Oddly, no. Maybe because they all know I'm Al's niece and one word from me and they're gone. But that's fine with me. Even though I'm only thirty, and do my best not to dress provocatively, I don't need a lot of catcalls and smart remarks because I walk up on men pounding nails into something. But they all do extremely good work and seem to be alright with me checking up on their work."

"Makes a big difference to the end product. No doubt about it. More and more women are proving they are just as good as men are when they pick up a hammer or saw. My mentor's daughter was almost as good as he was with tools."

"How did you get into making cabinets? You've only just started your business but you're a raging success already."

"It's a long story. Maybe later, when we have more time?"

She studied him for just a split second, "I love these hamburgers, especially the ones with their special sauces on them, called the Extra Saucy Burger, and I'd love to have more time to get to know your story." She moved her dinner plate toward her. Picking at her fries with her fork, she shuffled them over and over. When she finally looked up Talon smiled at her. "Dinner Friday night?"

"Perfect." Giving him her phone number and address, they left the diner. As she dropped him off back at his shop, Mariah turned toward him, "I really look forward to Friday night." All Talon could find himself doing, as he closed her car door, was give her a bright smile and a thumb's up sign.

Pulling away from the parking lot Mariah couldn't help but wonder what it was that kept Talon changing the subject or dodging the answers. He seemed nice enough, but there were obvious skeletons lurking in the background and she wasn't sure she would want to go beyond Friday night. It didn't escape her that she had one or two skeletons in her own closet. Everyone had some, of course, and she was no exception. No need to dwell on the past. She couldn't change it and had no desire to change it. She didn't even want to forget it. Learning experiences were very important in life. Still, there was an unsettling feeling in the pit of her stomach. She had to brush it off as an irrational fear. She hadn't dated in so many years she wasn't sure she even remembered how to do it.

Walking into the office he heard Anna humming a little tune. Her sharp eyes looked at him and she smiled. "So, when's the date?"

Talon actually felt himself blushing. "Ah, Friday. Dinner. I'll find some place neat to take her.

"Try Waterman's Grill in Virginia Beach. That would require a forty-five-minute drive each way, so you two can get to know each other better."

"I'll check it out," he replied. "Thanks."

Chapter 5

He was worse than a woman, changing clothes three times before settling on a suit. Waterman's Surfside Grill, in Virginia Beach, was his selection for the evening. It was just prior to tourist season so would be a lovely diversion with a fabulous view of the ocean. Then he changed his clothing again. Waterman's Surfside Grill was casual clothing. He liked that. Quickly sending a message to Mariah he advised her that dressing up for the dinner wasn't necessary, but the location was a surprise.

Double checking her address he pulled up at 7 P.M. When she opened the door he knew, once and for all, that he was looking at the most beautiful woman he had ever seen.

"You look smashing," he said.

"You said casual, so I thought this would be alright."

"It's perfect," he said, as she locked the door to her house, and he led her to his car.

He loved the forty-five-minute drive from Suffolk to the Virginia Beach oceanfront. Most of their conversation was light, with questions about construction and building and things they liked. By the time he turned the keys over to the valet they knew they had a mutual love of programs about the universe, mystery movies, 3-meat pizza, and vanilla ice cream!

"I've never eaten here before," She was in awe of the view as they sat down.

"Five-star rating, no less." Selecting the She Crab soup for the appetizer, Talon opted for the Ginger Soy Salmon for his main dinner, and Mariah decided on the Overstuffed Fish Bake. The food was so good they barely had time to talk between bites. Mostly they laughed and giggled, watching out the window at the surf and ships on the horizon.

Talon kept glancing up at her. Mesmerized would be a good word for what he felt with each glance. Her skin was smooth and clear, until she smiled. Then he saw two beautiful dimples. In the three times he'd seen her she hadn't worn any makeup at all. She didn't need it.

"I'd like to get to know you," said Talon. "You told me your dad had died and your mom is in Cleveland. Do you have any siblings?"

"Just one brother. He's married and lives in Richmond. I try to get up there every now and then to see them."

"What does he do for a living?"

"He's a pharmacist. He's four years older, and a super nice guy."

"I'll hope to meet him someday then."

Mariah smiled as she turned to take in the view out the window next to their table. "Yes. My sister-in-law, Sandy, is an accountant and they have a beautiful 13-year-old son named Ryan."

"Maybe we can drive up there some day. I've never been to Richmond. He's four years older, you say. Other siblings?"

"No. He's it. He's 34 now, but very successful and a loving husband and father. He and Sandy married right out of college. She worked very hard to support him for the four years he needed to go to pharmacy school. It was worth it in the end though. What about you? Any siblings?

"I have three brothers. Declan is local. He runs a company that invents medical equipment. I have two other brothers up in Pennsylvania.

Folding his napkin and placing it beside his plate he suddenly had a great idea. "How about we walk barefoot on the beach when we're done with dinner."

"*Great* idea. I'll need to walk off about 600 calories," she laughed as she picked up her water glass for a toast. "To the ocean walk," she toasted.

"May it be footprints in the sand," replied Talon.

Shoes safely tucked under a bench, they crossed the boardwalk and walked into the sand.

"OH, WOW," Suddenly Mariah started twirling in the sand, hands in the air, going in circles and advancing toward the ocean. Sticking her toes into the tidal water, "Whee!" Then, looking behind she saw Talon standing there as stiff as a statue. "Oh, Talon, I'm so sorry. I just suddenly felt like I was ten years old again. Would you rather we go?"

Walking up to where she stood, "Not a chance." Holding out his arms, "Dance with me in the sand and water." Bringing her into his arms he started to sway with her, losing himself in the smell of her hair and the lightness of her feet. Opening his eyes, he gazed into hers. "I'm not sure this should be happening to me, Mariah," putting his forehead down to meet hers.

"Yes, I know. Maybe too much, *way* too soon."

"You are so beautiful," he whispered.

Catching her breath, she tensed. This was unexpected. A dinner date was one thing, but him telling her she was beautiful, and with his face so close to hers...*take a deep breath, Mariah, and don't overthink anything. He's nice. He's gorgeous. But something isn't quite right.*

"And you are the most handsome man I've even set eyes on," she replied, pulling her head back and grinning at him.

Leading her from the sand and retrieving their shoes they started the drive back to Suffolk.

Had something shifted suddenly? Talon sensed that Mariah had gotten quiet and maybe a little distracted. While she let him hold her hand, she wasn't grasping his, just letting him hold it. While he searched his mind to figure out if he'd said something wrong, he couldn't come up with anything at all. He'd told her she was beautiful. Nothing wrong with that. Was there?

"Your head is stuck to that window, Mariah! What are you looking at so intently?"

"The stars. You don't see much of them here in the city. It's what I love about Suffolk. You can even see the Milky Way some nights."

"You sound almost wistful."

"Hmm, yes. I guess I do. When I was a child I used to sleep out in the backyard, on a blanket, with another one to cover me, and a pillow. I'd watch the stars all night. I woke up once and couldn't understand where the moon had gone. I mean, it was right up there directly in front of me when I fell asleep, and now it was gone. I sat up and looked around and noticed that now it was the same moon...you know, the man in the moon was still there...but it was behind me. That became my first 'astronomy' lesson from my dad. Rotation and Revolution. I was fascinated. He told me the next night to watch and see which 'stars' were blinking, and which were not. That was my second lesson. Stars, like our sun, blink. Planets do not." She sighed. "I almost swore I would be an astronomer when I grew up!"

"I have to admit, I knew that about the moon revolving around earth, but I never knew about the stars blinking. That's interesting," he said, taking one hand off the wheel to scratch his head.

"There's always so much to see and it depends on the time of year and the tilt of the earth."

"What's your favorite thing to find in the nighttime sky?"

"Oh, easy! Orion. I love September. I wait anxiously for September, because Orion is again my friend. Until February. Seems unfair to only have it for four or five months out of the year. And with all the new things they have learned about the universe, it's totally impossible to understand the rotation of our solar system as it swirls within the rotation and revolution of the Milky Way Galaxy. I struggle with all that."

Nodding, "I'm a big dipper fan myself, but then, that's the only thing I could ever find."

She laughed. "You should read up on the myth of Orion and how it came to be that his 'picture' is in the sky. It's fascinating."

"Well, maybe when September rolls around again you can point him out to me."

"That would be fun," she said, as Talon pulled into her driveway.

Taking his hand as he put the car in park and shut off the engine, "I had a very nice time tonight, Talon. Thank you," Quickly opening the door, she raced into her house, leaving Talon sitting there wondering where he had gone wrong. She hadn't even waited for his response.

It seemed that something had gone off the tracks, but for the life of him he couldn't figure out what he'd said or done that caused her to bolt like that. He pinched his nose trying to remember everything he had done, but nothing came to mind that would have upset her. Maybe she just figured out she didn't like him since he didn't get all excited when she started twirling in the sand. Whatever. He'd have to replay that evening in his mind. There was more than one thing he couldn't quite put his finger on right at that moment.

The weekend was long. He wished he had thought to ask her out again, much earlier in the evening. She'd bolted from the car so soon he didn't know what to make of it. All he had done, he thought, was show her a nice time, at a nice restaurant, and they even had a relaxing walk on the beach for a few minutes. Maybe he shouldn't have taken her in his arms on the first date. Was he wrong to tell her she was beautiful? They talked about the universe and it all seemed to be going alright. He was at a loss. He thought about driving over to Declan's and maybe talking to one of them about what happened, but he chickened out. He didn't want them to worry about him. Declan might have told him to ask Mariah out for a date, but he wasn't aware that they had gone out for one. He slogged through the weekend, doing the exercises the doctor had given him for his knee, and working on more furniture designs. He really wanted to get into more furniture than just cabinets, but for now at least cabinets were paying the bills. To kill time, he watched back to back football games on Sunday, finally falling asleep with thought of Mariah swirling through his mind.

Anna was waiting for him on Monday morning. He knew she would be, and it was only fair that he tell her how much they enjoyed the dinner at Waterman's.

"Before you bust a blood vessel, Anna, Waterman's is a fantastic restaurant and we had a great time. Even went for a walk on the beach. Thank you for the recommendation."

"And?"

"And, what?"

"Will you see her again?"

"I hope so. There's no new date on the horizon right now though."

"I'm sure you'll come up with something before long."

Talon just smiled back at her and headed toward the workroom. "I sure hope so," he shouted over his shoulder. Still, he couldn't seem to scratch the itch of what it was that bothered him.

Mariah paced. He as so handsome she could hardly breathe just thinking about him. Worst of all she had acted like an idiot, running from the car the second he stopped it in her driveway. How many years had it been since her last date? A dozen years? Something close to that. Her trust had been rock bottom. It was easier to live alone and be single than try to figure out the motives of men. They lied. They cheated, and they ran. There was something about Talon that bothered her. He seemed older. There had to be history. Divorced? It wasn't likely he was gay. Maybe with another date or two she would be able to figure out what bothered her so much. She couldn't be falling for him so soon. Despite his obvious gorgeous looks and strong, well-honed physique, she couldn't be falling under his spell so soon. Could she? *The only intelligent thing to do, Mariah, is try another date or two and see how it goes. You need to find out more."*

Wednesday, it was hard to believe it was now two and a half weeks since he'd dropped Mariah off at her house. There had been no contact between them. He debated calling her, many times, but she had rushed out so suddenly he was sure she couldn't get away fast enough. He ran that last evening they had shared, over and over, and could not figure out what he had done that was so wrong that she would feel the need to escape. Should he call her? Message her? Why should he have to do anything when she was the one that bolted? If he had done something to offend her then she should have spoken up and told him about it. As much as she made his heart rate go nuts, he had to acknowledge that she might be too much to deal with. She might be the emotional type, going bonkers over every little thing. Or maybe she was scared, but he never gave her any reason to be afraid of him. Did he? As often as he played that night over and over in his mind he knew, in the meantime, life must move on. He had a business to run and didn't want to mess it up in any way. He'd already spent twenty or so days thinking more about her than advancing his business.

Walking into his office, Anna stood up and handed him a note.

"Aaron gave this to me. Supplies he needs."

"Okay, I'll go down to Lowe's in a minute."

Walking into the shop he checked all the work being done. There wasn't any reason on earth to follow-up on any of the work that Aaron and Jacob did. It was so superior to his own efforts that he felt he could turn the whole place over to them without looking back!

"Anything else you two need?" he asked both Aaron and Jacob.

"You might start thinking about bringing in more help," suggested Aaron. "Starting to get just a tiny bit backlogged with all the work orders we're getting. Wife appreciates I'm working again, but she likes me home on time for dinner."

Talon chuckled, "I'll certainly check that out." Walking back into the office he asked Anna for a look at the incoming work orders. He was amazed at the increase in just a couple of days. Yes. More workers had to be something he would put on his priority list.

"I'll be at Lowe's, Anna."

"Ah, I've been watching and waiting, and if you don't mind my asking, what happened with that date you had with Mariah? You've seemed a bit withdrawn for the past couple of weeks."

Shrugging his shoulders, "She bolted, and I have no idea why. I didn't even try to kiss her!"

Giving Talon a sympathetic look, "I'm sorry, Talon. You're a super guy and maybe she'll come around."

"Catch you later," he said. With a sigh he opened the door and walked out to his truck.

With a couple of things on his hardware list he headed off to Lowe's. Gathering the saw blades and drill bits he needed he turned to head for the registers when he felt his elbow bump into something. Hearing a crash of things falling on the floor he turned quickly to see Mariah. He had knocked several packages of nails from her hands.

"Mariah!" Gathering his wits, "I'm sorry."

Mariah stood there looking at him, surprised to see him and unable, for some reason, to say anything.

Bending down to pick up the packages of nails for her he placed them in her basket then turned to leave for the registers. He did his best not to look into her eyes. She was as beautiful as ever, but he couldn't risk his emotions again. The only conclusion he could come to was that she had to be involved with someone else and had made her choice, for whatever reason, as they danced on the sand, smelled the ocean waters and felt the offshore breezes as they gently passed over them.

He stared at her for a moment, but she said nothing. It was like she was frozen to the floor. Giving her a questioning glance, he slowly pointed his finger at her, and with a quick sigh and clucking sound coming from his mouth he turned and walked away.

Going to the self-checkout he quickly swiped his card then got into his truck. But not fast enough. As he was fastening his seat belt there was a tap on his window. He jumped, then turned to see Mariah standing there, in the rain, getting soaked. He wound down the window. "Talon, are you okay?"

"Yes, of course I am. What can I do for you, Mariah?"

"Can we talk?"

"Is there something you need?"

"I'd like to know why?"

"Why what? Listen I need to get this stuff back to the shop and you are getting soaked." This was extremely uncomfortable for him. She didn't say anything to him for days. She hadn't called or texted. She hadn't visited his workspace. She hadn't said a word to him inside Lowe's. What was he supposed to think? Now she's banging on his car door wanting to talk? Asking why? Why *what?* Forget it. Not worth the trouble.

"I don't have the time now, Mariah. You're the one that bolted from my car and barely thanked me for dinner, when? Oh, yes. A couple of weeks ago. And not a word from you since then. Sorry. I need to get back to the shop."

Putting the truck into gear he slowly began moving forward as he closed the window. His last site of her seemed to be one of her arms raised, outstretched, palms up, and asking "*why?*"

Yeah, WHY? What the hell was that all about? She was the one who leaped out of his car and raced into her home. Without a word except saying she had a nice time. He guessed he had just simply moved too fast. So, okay. Lesson learned. It wouldn't happen again. Now to get back to work and get her out of his mind.

It was taking more effort than he expected to stop his fixation on Mariah, but he was succeeding. Probably because after that little demonstration he was more than a little annoyed. Or, as he would have said back in the old days in Pennsylvania, he was, quite frankly, pissed!

Another week rolled by and there was a needed delivery to one of Al's current sites.

"I got everything loaded, Talon," yelled Jacob, his head wrapping around the opened door to the shop. "You know where it has to go?"

"Yes. I'll be right there, Jacob."

"Maybe you should let Jacob handle this one alone, Talon," advised Anna.

53

"He'd get lost. Aaron left me a note, so I'll have to play navigator."

"Keep smiling, sport."

"Cute, Anna. I'll do my best," he gave her a thumb's up.

With Aaron out with a family problem he was needed to at least get the load to the site, where some of Al's workers would unload. As he drove, he was hoping it was a site with a different supervisor in charge. A man could hope. He didn't need any more stress.

Unloading, and turning to help haul in the first table he saw Mariah, directing them to the correct room. Her head was down, avoiding him to the best of her ability. Jacob nodded to her with an added "Good morning Miss Mariah," and she lifted her head long enough to glance at him and give him a smile.

"Good morning, Jacob. As usual the furniture is gorgeous. Outstanding craftsmanship, and our clients are thrilled."

"Thank you, Miss Mariah. I'll be sure to let Aaron know."

As the rest of the cabinets were being taken into the home, the van now empty, Talon walked out to begin the trip back to his shop, but found Mariah blocking the door to his van.

Frustrated, "What do you want, Mariah? I figured you had all you could stand of me what? Three weeks ago. No, maybe four. Just open the car door and race into your house with nothing more than a 'had fun' comment. Really was glad to know you appreciated the food and walk in the sand, not to mention the dance in the tide." Reaching for the door handle, she blocked him again.

"I need to know why, Talon."

"What the blazes are you talking about?" His face was turning red and he was getting angrier by the second. "You blow me off and then want to know *why*? *why WHAT*?"

"You haven't called me."

"You have to be kidding."

She just stared at him. "Like I just said, you couldn't wait to get out of the car and rush into your house. With an astronomy lesson on the entire trip back from Virginia Beach, no less. What the hell am I supposed to think? Seems to me like you didn't have all that great a time and couldn't wait to get away from me."

"It wasn't like that."

"Well I sure as… never mind. It's what I remember."

"You scared me."

"*What*? Are you *SERIOUS*? I never even tried to kiss you while we were dancing, for god's sake. Just dancing scares you?"

"It was too soon to be liking you as much as I did."

He stared at her, his eyes still blazing, and his mouth open ready to spit out more angry words, but she had just stunned him. "Excuse me!"

"I was afraid. I don't believe that love can happen that quickly, that I kept thinking that I was just attracted to you, ah, well, your good looks and all that. But all I do is think about you, all day, all night. I…"

It was pure impulse to take that half step forward and pull her in for a kiss. And not just any old kiss. Releasing her she stumbled and nearly fell. "WOW," was all she could say as he caught her.

"Fine. You be scared, and I won't be scared. The ball's in your court." Reaching over he physically picked her up and moved her from his truck, got in and drove away.

Women, he thought. Geeze. Nothing but trouble. Slamming his fist on the steering wheel, he realized that Jacob was with him and probably curious about the entire event he just witnessed.

"You okay, man?" asked Jacob.

"I'm working on it."

"Miss Mariah has you twisted in knots, huh?"

"Seems that way and I hate to admit it. You married, Jacob?"

"Yup. Going on 30 years now."

"Do you understand your wife?"

"Nope. Not any of my four daughters either. I just bring home the paycheck and let them do their doings around me."

Talon chuckled. "But are you happy?"

"Never been happier. Course, we have our moments, kinda like what you just went through back there, but it's those kisses to make up that are worth it all in the end."

Pulling into the shop parking lot, "Time will tell, Jacob, time will tell."

"Yes sir. I'll just git on back to work now."

"Thanks, Jacob. Hopefully Aaron will be able to get back here by tomorrow."

"You look worse now than you did when you left," observed Anna.

"You wouldn't believe it, Anna."

"Try me."

"Mariah was there."

"And…"

"She told me she ran into the house because I scared her. She was feeling too much for me too soon, or something like that. So, I gave her a gigantic kiss then left, leaving the ball in her court!"

Talon didn't see her smile, "I do believe you'll be hearing from her," was all Anna could say. "I'll be interested in how she accomplishes that little chore."

"I'll be sure to keep you advised of the timeline regarding my love life," Talon looked sideways at Anna.

"I'm not going anywhere. Don't forget, I have two grown children. Hard to put one over on me. God knows they tried," she snorted. "You're easier to read than they ever were."

Ah, geeze, Talon. Nothing like being transparent!

Now he was thoroughly confused. He had never dealt with a woman on this level. She bolts because she's afraid she's feeling too much for him. That was just ridiculous. After one date. Stupid. He wanted to get to know her better. She was beautiful. But to react like that after one date just seemed to be a bit over the top. Past experience was no help. All his past 'girlfriends' chased him. He didn't have to put any effort into getting their attention at all. He wondered if it would do him any good to talk to Em. Not likely Declan would have any clue, but she might.

He called her. "Hey, Em. Any chance I can come over and bounce Cailen around for a bit?"

Good. She said he could come over.

"I'll be there after I close up shop."

Maybe, if he was lucky, the chef had made enough food for their dinner. Then he could get a good meal for a change. Microwave meals were okay, but there was a limit to how many days in a row he could handle that stuff.

"Cailen. I swear you've grown six inches since I left."

Cailen giggled, bringing a smile to the faces of both Em and Talon.

"He is such a cutie. You two are going to have your hands full when he gets to high school and catches the eye of every girl in the building."

"I know. I've even thought about that, believe it or not."

"Well, maybe with some luck," he raised Cailen up to the ceiling and quickly brought him back down, to the excited squeal of his nephew, "he'll be more like Declan than me."

"Or some kind of cross between those two extremes," she offered, putting her hands in prayer mode.

Talon sat down in the family room, bouncing Cailen on his knee. "I love that giggle he has," he said.

"He adores you; you know. All I have to do is say your name and he gets a smile on his face."

Talon leaned back, cradling Cailen in his arms.

"I have a question, Em. I need some insight into the feminine mind."

"Oh really?"

"Hmm. Yes."

"I'll do my best. How can I help?"

"I don't know if Declan shared this with you, but I took a woman named Mariah out on a date to dinner. It went well. I drove her home and she bolted from the car and raced inside before I could even say goodnight to her."

"Did you say anything to upset her?"

"Nope. We talked about the stars and planets and moon all the way home."

"Did she get quiet the closer you got to her place?"

Talon stopped to think. "Yeah, I guess you could say that."

"Then she was scared. I would guess she was afraid you might want a good night kiss, or even to come in for a minute, or something along that line, and she was afraid of how she would react to it."

"But I didn't do anything or say anything to frighten her, Em. I swear it."

"Well, it's more the expectations she was worried about. The unknown. She might have been hoping you'd kiss her, yet afraid you would. You'll have to get to know her a bit better to find out the back story, but my guess is she's scared that she had discovered she likes you too much, too soon."

"I saw her again at a building site, and that's almost what she said to me."

"Take it for the truth then."

"I don't understand. I wasn't threatening her. I wasn't even going to kiss her, just walk her to the door and say goodnight. I'm really trying hard to get past my wicked ways."

"Nothing suggestive, in words or actions?"

"Nope. Well, I did tell her she was beautiful. She could probably hear my heart beating it was so loud."

Emily laughed. "I'd say she's very much attracted to you. Maybe she grew up thinking love had to develop slowly to mean anything. Maybe she's never had a lot of dates in her life, and Talon, you are one very handsome dude. She's probably afraid she'll fall at your feet and make an idiot out of herself. So, she has to make a quick exit to keep from grabbing you! You just need to build up some patience, Talon."

His look was quizzical.

"Call her for another date. Keep it simple and in public. Let her get to know you. Sounds like you care enough to try to figure out how to proceed, so feel free to bring her here sometime."

"Okay. I guess it sounds reasonable." Pausing to bounce Cailen around on his knees for a few seconds, "Thanks, Em."

"Anytime, Talon. I've told you before I think you're very special. I'd like nothing better than to see you happily married, bouncing your own kids on your knee. Ah. I hear Declan is here. Stay for dinner?"

"I'd love to."

Shouting, "I'm in here, Declan, with Talon. He had to come over and get a Cailen fix."

Chapter 6

Mariah had been pacing so much at work that Al finally walked up to her and stopped her in her tracks.

"Give it up, kid."

"What?"

"I said, why are you doing more pacing than working?"

"Am I not doing my job?"

"Are you avoiding my question, Mariah? Who is he?"

Folding her arms, defensively in front of her, "No one special, Uncle."

"So, you are going to make me play a guessing game?"

She sighed at him, then moved her mouth into a right-side grin, "No. It's Talon."

"I suspected as much but hadn't guessed it was Talon you were pining over. I do remember telling you he was a very handsome guy though!"

"Uncle Al!"

"Hey! He's a very handsome man. I can understand the attraction. You're a gorgeous woman. Time you found someone. You've been living in a cave for far too many years. So, keep on pacing and keep me posted."

"I just have some decisions to make. He's hiding something, and I'm not sure how serious it is. But I do have a plan. Just waiting for something I ordered to be delivered."

"Why do you think he's hiding something?"

"He's an older guy. I'm not sure how old he is. I know that sounds silly, but I'd expect – shoot, I don't know – maybe someone a bit more settled down with a relationship. He's drop dead gorgeous, as you have pointed out, and he's intelligent and talented. But I figure something isn't quite right. There's something in his past that defines him, and I guess until I find out what that is, I'm going to be a bit uncomfortable around him. Then again, it's not like I've had lots of dates in my life, so I might not have a clue and am just afraid I'll fall hard for him and he won't fall hard back. Does any of that make sense?"

"Nope. But I'm sure you realize that you have your own reasons for all these emotions. Everyone has a past, Mariah, including you. I'm just going to let you run with all that, and figure it out for yourself. But if you do find out he's an escaped prisoner, let me know, will you?"

Raising both hands into the air, "Chee!"

Two more weeks passed. Nothing. Maybe space and time were good things. Talon went home to his apartment every night, take-out dinner in hand. Maybe he should get a cat for company. Not a bad thought. But then there was the litter box. He sighed. Tomorrow Aaron and Jacob would be delivering the last of the cabinets for Al's current order. Probably for the better.

Walking into the office the next day, "How are we doing Anna? I've been so busy I haven't asked."

"Each month gets better and better, boss. and, you just got an order from Al for thirty more cabinets. Maybe you need to think about getting more help in the shop!"

Thirty more cabinets!!! "Holy smokes. I guess so. I'll see if Jacob or Aaron have any friends as good as they are, who might also like to have a job."

Talking to them Talon found they had four more men who would be perfect for his organization. "Tell them they start tomorrow then. Give their names to Anna and they can fill in the paperwork when they arrive. We have a *huge* order coming in."

Talon was excited. His business was not only good, it was taking off like a rocket. He might even have to rent the rest of the now defunct peanut factory and pull down a few walls.

Over the loudspeaker, Anna said, "Talon you have a package just arrived."

Walking into the office he spied a big box on the counter. The return address was Al Devon's Company. Opening it he burst into laughter. The ball was now back in his court. Inside the box was a very nice telescope and a book on astronomy. The ball had vaulted back into his court, and he was going to make the most out of it. It was nice weather outside. Warm. A blanket out, under the stars. Maybe on the far edge of Declan's property, and Declan did have a huge amount of land. His mind was racing, but before the afternoon was over, he had his plan.

Sending her a message:

Thank you for the telescope. Are you free for dinner Friday night? Casual.

The reply was almost immediate.

Yes, what time?

7 P.M.

See you then.

Calling Declan, he laid out a plan, and Declan agreed it would be a fun thing to do. Talon promised to stop by after work, and they could proceed with setting up the event for Friday evening. Declan and Emily would do a test run the night before to make sure it worked as intended. With luck the chef made enough dinner so he could stay for that too.

"So where are we going for dinner?"

"It's a surprise. Only about a ten-minute ride."

Pulling up to the gate, Talon rolled down the window, punched in a code, and the gates opened. Seeing the house as they approached, "Where are we?"

"My brother's."

"Ah, Alright, I guess."

"You'll love them."

Offering his hand to help her out of his car he could feel the tension in her body. Her hand was shaking, and her eyes belied her nervousness. "Honest to goodness, Mariah, they don't bite. The baby might *GUM* you, but he doesn't have teeth yet."

Mariah laughed, and visibly relaxed as Talon led her into the house.

"Declan! Em! We're here."

"In the kitchen, Talon," yelled Emily.

It seemed so comfortable to guide Mariah using his hand on the small of her back. "Hi, Em. Declan. May I introduce Mariah Rogers?" Mariah had tried to partially hide behind Talon, but he moved to give her full exposure to Declan and Emily.

Smiles and 'glad to meet you' abounded and Declan offered Mariah a chair. "We're rather informal here. Nothing fancy."

"Ah, yeah," murmured Mariah. "Except the whole house," She looked around in awe. "My whole house could fit into this kitchen."

"We're growing into all this space," offered Declan.

"Speaking of which, where's my nephew?"

"Cailen is sound asleep, and you just leave him be, Talon."

"Em, please."

"If you promise to go quietly, just look and do not pick him up, then go ahead."

Grabbing Mariah's hand, he led her upstairs to the nursery. They found Cailen sleeping on his back, both arms pointing toward the wall behind his head. True to his promise he didn't attempt to pick him up, but when Mariah was heard to say softly, "What a sweet baby," Talon couldn't resist. "He's a good boy and has the best parents a kid could want."

"I love the décor of the room too. Very masculine yet woodsy and filled with adventure. I'll bet it won't be any time at all before he can tell you the names of all the jungle animals painted on the wall."

"Declan told me Em is already reading him stories. Wouldn't surprise me to find out he's a genius by the age of three."

She laughed.

Returning just as dinner was served, they sat down to eat. Declan offered wine, but both Talon and Mariah declined. The rest of dinner was filled with the usual small talk and questions of where from, what job, parents, siblings. When she quietly asked Declan what he did she was very surprised to hear just exactly who he was. Looking at Talon, "I had no idea, you had a brother so talented and important," she said. "You told me what he did, but I hadn't put it all together."

Declan couldn't help but smile. "Mariah, I'm just a regular guy who got lucky and hired the right people. Now Emily here is a physical therapist. She's hoping soon that she can get back to doing that now that Cailen is growing. We'll hire a sitter to take care of him and she can go to work and worry every second about how he's doing back home without his mother around."

Emily gave him the evil eye. "Maybe I'll open my own therapy center right here in the house then!"

Declan gave her a funny look that Mariah didn't understand, and Talon cleared his throat, asking, "Any desert tonight, Em?"

"How about chocolate covered nails for the men, and tiramisu for us ladies?" She winked at Mariah as she stood to serve the desserts.

"Have you told Mariah the surprise yet?" asked Declan.

"That's next. She has no idea!"

"Then you two go ahead, and I'll clean up." Emily held up her hand as Mariah got up to help. "I think you'll be quite surprised, Mariah!"

Again, escorting Mariah out of the house she was confused when he led her out the back door.

"Declan's property is huge. Several acres. He has a gazebo down this path that you'll be interested in," Speaking slowly he began to realize how close Mariah was, walking next to him, their arms grazing in the darkness of night.

"It's totally dark. How can you see where you're going when it's so pitch black out here?"

"Guess I've done it so many times I know the path by heart. I lived with Declan and Emily for several months when I came down from Pennsylvania and used to come down and sit in the gazebo to gather my thoughts and find peace. Here," putting his arm around her waist, he was able to better guide her. After about thirty more steps, "Okay, we're here."

Flipping a switch on a tree, a small light glowed, and she could see the telescope she had sent to Talon, set up and ready to watch the stars. A blanket was anchored on the ground just beside it. Turning off the light he led her to the blanket. "Lie down and look up!"

"Oh, gosh. What a beautiful site. You can see thousands and thousands of stars. This is incredible."

"And feel free to look through the telescope," pointing to it as he settled down on the blanket, beside her.

"I can't believe you did all this. It's perfect. I could stay here all night watching the moon move across the sky. A nice breeze, temperatures are just right, the stars are bright and all's right with the world. Well, my world anyway."

"I'm sorry Orion isn't around yet."

"There's plenty to see regardless. Ursa Major. Ursa Minor. Leo. Virgo. Oh, this is just amazing." Turning toward Talon, "Thank you so much for this, Talon. This is the best surprise ever."

"Declan and I set it up yesterday and they tested it out last night while I watched Cailen. Declan was so impressed that he has ordered a gigantic telescope to put in a little hut, with reclining chairs, and, if I know Declan, it will have a bathroom and refrigerator. He tends to think of everything."

"I am green with envy."

Leaning up on his arm all he saw was beauty. His eyes had adjusted to the moonlight and he couldn't imagine anything more perfect than what he was seeing before him. His free hand moved to her chin, his thumb stroking her cheek. She didn't move. Lowering his head, he kissed her gently. Mariah raised her arm, placing her hand behind his neck, rubbing it carefully. Again, Talon stroked her cheek with his thumb, then quickly laid back down again beside her, his heart thumping so hard he feared it would come out of his chest. Reaching over he took her hand and held it tightly. She made no move to reject it. Instead she rolled over to his side, folding herself into his outstretched arm, "Just hold me Talon. Okay?"

"Okay." Talon paused for a minute, silently slowing his breathing, but unable to look down at her. "You're making me crazy, Mariah, and I have to be careful. I don't want to go back to what I've been in the past."

"Can you talk about it?"

"Not now. Maybe someday. For sure. Some day."

"That's alright. We all have things that are difficult to talk about."

Talon squeezed her hand, and Mariah rolled back to check out the stars once again.

Talon and Mariah became regulars at their favorite diner - that same diner where they had eaten lunch. Trying to meet every night, it was to be expected that they would have to skip an evening here or there. When they did manage to make it to the diner, Talon always took her back to her apartment but would give her a gentle kiss at the door, refusing to go inside. "I can't go in, Mariah. Not yet. I'm afraid I'd completely lose control and you're too precious for that."

While she seemed to understand he could sense her frustration. Of course, his frustration was beyond extreme. He was having a hard time behaving himself. It was absolutely the opposite of what he had done his entire adult life up to that point. But this "old dog" had to learn some new tricks, for sure. He wanted any moves he made on her to be sincere and mutual. No more one-nighters. No more love-em-and-leave-em, with no regrets on his part. He cared about her too much to lose control again.

Declan had planned an intimate July 4 evening, under the stars, with a small fireworks display, for just the four of them. But the news came late on the afternoon of the third.

Talon was just leaving work to meet Mariah, at the pub, where they would have dinner, when his phone rang. It was Braedon. That could not be good news. Answering the call, he was floored to hear that Bryce had just died. Black Lung Disease. Standing beside his car, stunned, he called Declan.

Telling him what had happened he could hear Emily in the background, "Declan?"

"Yes, Talon, I have Braedon on hold. God, this is awful."

Declan covered the speaker on the phone to tell Emily, "Bryce just died, well, late yesterday. The Black Lung disease finally got him. Talon just got a call from Braedon too."

Returning his attention back to the phone, "Hang on a second, Talon, and let me talk to Braedon again." After a short pause, "Okay, Talon. You want to ride up with us? Do you know when the funeral is?"

"Yes, and Yes. Braedon said the funeral is Friday."

"I was so shocked I either forgot to ask him or didn't hear. Then it looks like tomorrow is best. Can you leave the shop in your worker's hands?"

"OH, absolutely. Aaron and Jacob are both supervisors and each one of them has four other Amish gentlemen working for them. With Anna there, my life is a breeze now!"

"Let's plan on leaving from my house at 10 then. With Cailen it might take a bit longer and we'll have to stop for a good lunch on the way. Hold on a sec... What did you say Emily? Oh... Yes... I'll let him know."

Putting the phone back up to his ear, "Emily says we can all stay with her mom. She just got off the phone, so they will be expecting us. Maybe we can just plan to stay and come back Sunday. That will give Emily and Cailen lots of grand mom and aunt time. Sound Doable?"

"Sounds perfect. I'll see you tomorrow morning."

Talon sent a quick message to Mariah that he would be out of town for several days, then headed home to get packed. Throwing his phone on the charger he put clothing in his suitcase, his travel shaver, toothbrush and other soaps and after shave lotions, on and on. Then a quick shower and he went to bed, knowing the next few days he would need all the resources he could muster to return to Defiance, Pennsylvania. It was a bad night and sleep was hard to find. He wasn't sure he could go back to Defiance and survive the trip. Too many memories, heartbreaks, bad decisions, cold nights in the winter and blistering heat in the summer inside his shed... His thoughts were all consuming and completely divorced from his present-day life. Somehow, he would have to manage four more days of Defiance. Maybe, with luck, he could basically hide out at Em's mother's and just go to the funeral. He doubted any of his former ladies would show up at the funeral or the gathering, as he didn't know Bryce at that time of his life. They could have had mutual friends. He had no idea. Not really. Not until his father died anyway. Memories of those times scared him almost to death. With luck he could get through it all without going into a panic. He'd been given all the tools to keep himself safe from both women and booze. Hopefully, without asking, Declan and Em would be watching him to be sure nothing dramatic happened to send him back to his old ways. One day at a time. It was the best he could come up with for a battle plan.

Chapter 7

Waking a bit later than usual he grabbed his suitcase and hauled himself out the door. He made it just at the 10 A.M. stated time, and Emily and Declan were just exiting the house. Carefully placing Cailen in his little car seat, Talon took the back seat next to him. "Guess it's just us guys, Cailen," he mused.

Closing the gate behind them, "We'll just take 460 up to 295, then North on 95. It may seem slower, but we miss all the tunnel backups on the M&M and Hampton Roads Bridge Tunnel. Those are insane. It's one very good reason to live in Suffolk and not 30 miles east of here!"

Emily was sound asleep before they even got to Disputanta! Talon saw Declan smiling in the rear-view mirror. Lifting his hand and pointing his thumb toward his wife, he just shook his head. Talking was hard with the music playing, and Cailen kept beating his hands against his car seat like the little drummer boy. Talon had to laugh. Tapping Declan on the shoulder, "If you get tired after a couple hours, just wake me up. Otherwise we'll switch at lunch." Declan gave him a thumb's up. Scrunching down in his luxury Lincoln seat it didn't take him long to go to sleep either.

Three hours down the road, Talon was rudely awakened by "Okay, folks, everyone out of the pool. Lunch time."

Tapping his wife on the arm, she tried to roll over, but was unsuccessful. Tapping her again and she opened her eyes, suddenly realizing where they were. "How's Cailen doing?"

"Not a peep out of him so far. In fact, his little eyes are as closed as the other passengers in this car," snarked Declan.

"Be nice, husband, or I'll file for divorce."

"That will be the day!"

And, as usual, the loving smile she shot back at him was all he needed to mouth '*I love you*' back to her. Coming around to her side of the car he carefully took his sleepy son from the car seat, and all went inside for lunch.

While Emily took Cailen into the lady's room, to change his diaper, Declan and Talon found a booth and sat down. They made sure there was a highchair waiting when Emily returned.

Lunch was silent. Emily fed Cailen the baby food she had brought along, and the somberness of their trip was beginning to take hold of their spirits. All three ate their sandwiches quietly, lost in thought.

Gathering up the paper plates and napkins for disposal Declan couldn't help but comment. "I'm really getting sad by all these funerals. Three in so short a time. I hope this is the end of them for a very long time."

"I agree," said Talon, his voice low. "I'm not the least bit comfortable to going back to Defiance. Hoped to never set foot in that town again."

Emily watched as Declan picked up his son and they headed out to the car. They were right. It was great that they would get to see her mom, sister and niece, but she understood only too well what they were saying.

"How bout I finish the drive, Declan?"

"Yes, that would be fine. Hopefully Cailen will go back to sleep and I can catch a few zzzzz's too. Or," turning to Emily, "Would you rather sit in the back with Cailen?"

"Yes. You take the front with Talon."

It was 4 P.M., almost exactly, when Talon pulled up to the Steele home. Emily's mom rushed out the door and demanded to be given her grandson! Emily handed him over immediately. "Okay, you can go back home now," she glowed, rocking her grandson. "Just leave Cailen here." Her smile was infectious, and Emily was thrilled. When Dawn and Sherry ran over from their house next door, all Sherry wanted to do was hold her new cousin. "Mom, he's *adorable*," she gushed. Dawn had to agree, while giving her sister a huge hug. "We're so glad you're here, just very sad that it's for another funeral. You have *got* to plan a visit when it's a happy time."

"Hi, Paula," Declan walked up to Emily's mom and gave her a hug. "Lord, Declan, you get better looking every time I see you." Giving him a brief kiss on the cheek, she turned, "and WOW, Talon. I would *never* have recognized you. No kidding."

Talon blushed at the compliment, but pointing toward Declan and Emily, "I owe it all to them. If they hadn't taken control of me after I got out of rehab, I rather expect I would have just gone back to the old life – it was the only life I knew."

"Then thank God, Talon. You really do look super. Let's go in. I have some food ready, and believe it or not, Emily, Jack is here this time. He's been so busy at work he never gets off, but Dawn convinced him to take a few days leave while you are all here. He was a good husband and said he would." She grinned.

As they entered the house introductions were made all around, and everyone helped to bring in the luggage, except Sherry, who wasn't about to give up her cousin so easily. "She's good with kids," whispered Dawn to her sister. "Babysits a lot around here, so you can trust her completely."

"Emily, you and Declan take the Master, as it has the private bath. That way you can change Cailen with no problems. Is it alright if Cailen stays in the same room? I borrowed a crib for him."

"Totally perfect, Mom. But we hate to run you out of the Master."

"A bed is a bed. I will take your old room and Talon can have Dawn's. Can you handle a pink bedroom for a few days, Talon?" she grinned.

"I'll just turn off the lights and go to sleep," he promised, chuckling more to himself than the room of people.

Sitting down to a bowl of chili and crackers followed by an apple pie for dessert, all were sated and comfortable.

"Have you heard the arrangements for Bryce?" asked Declan.

"The funeral is Friday and then there's a gathering at his home. That gives you tomorrow to rest up, and the weekend to just do whatever you want to do before you go back." Paula was already sounding wistful about their upcoming departure.

Emily looked at Declan and noticed that he was withdrawn, silently standing and twirling his thumbs. "Are you okay, Declan?" she whispered.

"Yes. It's just hard to know I am burying a brother who's 68 now, and I've only known him for the past year."

"He was very sick," added Paula. "When I talked to Madison, she said he had been having severe breathing problems for the past month. He's at peace now, Declan. The coal mines got him, but hopefully he's the last one in our family to die so horribly."

Emily stood up from the table and took her son in her arms. "We're off to bed, Mom. Cailen is beyond tired, and I'm starting to droop myself."

"Let me know if you need anything."

Declan remained in his chair for a bit. "Takes her awhile to get him bathed, into his bed clothing and settled down." Turning toward Talon, "You okay brother?"

"Yeah. Doing alright. Tired like the rest of you, but I'll make it."

Motioning for Jack to stand up, "Well, we're going to head home," Dawn said, as she crooked her finger at Sherry, "So you guys can all get a good night's rest." Picking up the last of the dirty dishes Dawn moved toward the sink, and then the door. Her husband and daughter were right on her heels.

Declan sipped on his coffee; his legs stretched out before him as he relaxed.

"Anything else I can get you two?" asked Paula.

"I'm more than fine," answered Declan.

"Same here, thanks," added Talon.

Shifting to a sitting up position, "I do have a question, though," Declan turned toward Paula.

"Ask away."

"I should be keeping up with stuff like this, but what's going on with our, well mom's house?"

"I guess when you were here for her funeral, you'd hired a company to update it. At least that's what I was told."

"Yes. Wanted to get it ready to sell."

"All of that work has been completed. But as far as I know that's been the end of it. We've had our lawn mowing company go ahead and do the yard all summer, to keep it looking nice, but to tell you the truth I just really hadn't thought much about the house at all. It never occurred to me to ask Emily about it when we talked on the phone. All we even talked about was Cailen," she confessed, sheepishly.

"Then nothing has been done past that time. To sell it?"

"Not that I know of. Like I said, I just haven't really thought about it, Declan."

"I'm sorry, Paula. I really should have been more alert to what was going on. I'll be more than happy to pay you for all the yard mowing, and anything else you might have done to keep the place up to snuff."

"It wasn't, and isn't, a problem, Declan. Honestly. It only needed mowing a couple of times. We've been in a drought here, so the grass hasn't been growing very fast. Now that fall is here there won't be any problems at all with it."

"Hey," Declan looked over at Talon, who was just sitting there in silence, "It's still light outside. You want to go check out the house and see what shape it's in?"

"Sure, why not."

"Maybe while we're all here we can get a realtor over and put it up for sale."

"A good idea. There's really no one left in the family that would want to live in it."

All three of them stood at the same time, and Declan and Talon left as Paula turned to put the dishes in the dishwasher.

"We won't be long, Paula," said Declan.

"Take your time. I don't go to bed until around ten or so, and I'll leave the door unlocked for you. Just lock up when you come back."

Walking across the grass they both stopped at a couple of spots to get a good view of the house. The rotting wood had been replaced and the fresh coat of paint gleamed in the setting sun.

"Sure looks different," observed Talon.

"Yeah, not bad."

"Maybe I should have gone ahead and done siding instead of new wood," mused Declan.

"It looks good like it is. It's good for several years now."

"Let's check out the back."

Shuffling through the new mown grass, "Paula must have had it mowed today. You can still smell the fresh grass cuttings."

"Yes. Nice. I do see we should probably get all the weeds taken out of the flower beds."

"Or just eliminate the flower beds all together."

"Another good thought."

Then Talon stopped so suddenly that Declan nearly ran into him.

"What?" he asked his brother.

"Oh, my God," Talon answered.

Declan looked left to right, not seeing anything dangerous or particularly out of order. "What?" he asked again.

"The shed is gone."

Declan focused. "Seriously, Talon?"

Talon was silent, just staring at the spot where the shed had stood.

"You doing alright, brother?"

"Maybe it's for the best," he said softly. "Maybe there are some things in history that need to just go away."

Declan reached up and patted his brother on the back. "I understand. Sometimes when I think about how close I came to losing Emily it makes my blood run cold. It's in the past, Talon. You need to move forward. Use those memories to punch ahead, not drag you back."

"Yeah. You're right. Did you bring a key for the house?"

Declan wiggled his key chain. "Oddly enough I've had the key on my key chain since Dad died. Mom gave it to me when I set up all the remodeling. Never thought to take it off."

They took a long stroll through the house, pleased with the final appearance of every room.

"Weird to walk through an empty house," said Talon.

Declan walked to the window that had been along the back wall of his room. "They put new screens in too. The holes are gone. I used to watch bugs come in and out through those holes," he huffed. "No need to even open the windows now that there's a brand new air conditioning system installed."

"Everything seems to be done."

"Yes. And it does look good. I'm happy with the results. I'll have to let the contractors know I'm pleased and then settle the bill. Then I can set it up with a realtor. We'll have to figure out how to divvy up the money after it's sold."

"My bank account is getting stronger, Declan, and you sure don't need another dime. Braedon is doing well. Maybe we can just help out Bryce's family. He was a coal miner. That was never a well-paying job."

"Agree. Maybe we can find out more when we visit Madison, and I'll make sure Braedon is alright with it."

Chapter 8

When Thursday morning arrived both Declan and Talon agreed they should drive over to see Madison. Declan had talked to Emily when they got up and asked her if she wanted to go. She had declined, thinking a baby wouldn't fit in too well, and Sherry was in school. She would be happy just sitting around the kitchen catching up with her mom. Unless, of course, he preferred or needed her. Assuring her that it was fine for her to stay home, he and Talon left.

They both let out deep breaths upon arrival. All the way over Declan could only remember the childhood he had gone through. The known fact that his brother had done nothing to help him was always going to be a sore point. He could forgive, knowing the cause, but he could never forget. Years of starvation and brutality at the hands of his parents, with Talon heaping even more abuse upon him… it made him shiver just thinking about those years. Talon was responsible for so many problems in Declan's life, but at least that was over. Now that he understood how his parents had blamed all those involved in the baseball game that killed his brother, years before he was born, he could accept that they had all been victims.

"Ready?"

"I guess so," answered Talon.

Gently knocking on the door, Madison opened it and bade them to enter.

"We just wanted to make sure you were alright and being cared for," began Declan, as he gave Madison a hug. Talon followed with his own hug and soon they were joined by the three children. They all seemed to have accepted it, knowing at least that Bryce's suffering was over.

"He was so very sick," Madison shared. "His lungs were no longer operating. He was on oxygen 24 hours a day. He couldn't eat much and had lost almost a quarter of his weight. We all loved him, and miss him, but we also agree that the only way we would want him back is if he was healthy. Not suffering as he did. It was truly awful to watch him suffer so horribly."

"I'm sorry we didn't know he was so sick," Talon said. "We could have come up for visits, as well as get him any extra help you might need to care for him."

"We were able to get him excellent hospice care for the last two weeks. It helped tremendously. Gave me a break from the constant worry," said Madison, "but also enabled pain medications so he could rest peacefully. We were all here when he died. He knew how much we loved him."

All three children sat down on the sofa with their mom and agreed. They also assured Declan and Talon that their mom would be well cared for. There was a nice insurance policy that would help her financially, and they were all located close by to give her any needed support.

"Declan, and Talon," Madison continued, "We know that for years he was haunted by the story of your childhood years. He just hoped, in the end, that you had forgiven both him and Braedon. When she started crying, both Declan and Talon assured her that they had indeed forgiven their brothers, and that if Madison ever needed anything that the kids couldn't handle all she had to do was call either of them. They had the children make the same promise. "We're family," assured Declan. "Don't ever be embarrassed to ask for anything you need."

All of them nodded their heads in gratitude.

"I do want you to know," continued Declan, "that Talon and I have agreed to put Mom's house up for sale in the next couple of days. It's finished and ready. I'll personally see to it that the money from the sale is transferred to your account, Madison. Mom left the house to her four sons, and Talon, Braedon and I have plenty of money. All of us agreed we want to ensure that you have all you need to live out the rest of your life in comfort."

Madison dabbed tears from her eyes. "I accept your kindness, Declan, because I know it's from your heart and you are well set for life. All of you will be in my daily prayers, and I truly hope if you come back to visit, for any reason, that you know you're always welcome in my home."

With hugs all around Declan and Talon left, feeling much better about the visit, and were now more certain than ever that they had lost a very dear brother.

"I didn't know you had talked to Braedon about selling the house," said Talon.

"I haven't. Yet. He'll be fine with it. He's worth millions. He offered to help me pay for all the stuff we had done to the house, but I told him I was worth more than him, so he bowed to my extreme wealth." Declan was chuckling. "But I will call him to make it a given."

"Seems I have some catching up to do, then, if I want to compete with you two."

"Yup. Start making furniture too. That should do it."

Buckling his seat belt, "Yes. I like that idea," noted Talon.

Heading back to Paula's, "She's a lovely lady," observed Talon. "I wish all of us could have had more time together. It just seems all we do is meet over funerals. Well, your wedding, but then you and Em abandoned all of us to go on your honeymoon." Talon was smiling his usual wicked smile that had made him so popular with the ladies all his life.

"Thank God she has the three kids to help her. They seem to be good kids. Bryce had good insurance, so she won't need help, at least not yet, and the money from selling the house will probably secure her future, but I hope they all really understand that it will only take a phone call to me if they ever need any kind of special help." Declan's hands were wrapped tightly around the steering wheel. "We need to schedule some reunions, like every six months."

Pulling back into the Steele driveway, Talon got out and tapped on top of the car, drumming his fingers, "I think I'll go for a walk down to Defiance Station or something. I just need some thinking time."

"A bit of exercise too, I'd imagine. Are you still doing the knee exercises?"

"Up until yesterday, yes. Knee is much better, so it probably won't make any difference if I don't do them anymore. Em was right, as usual. I need to be more careful if I want to keep walking on two legs."

"Okay, don't be late for lunch, though. Paula is really going all out to take care of us. Why not go inside and see if she needs anything while you're going there!"

"Good idea, Got it."

Paula was good with no grocery list. Wandering down to the store, Talon figured he'd better send a message to

Mariah, to let her know exactly what was happening. He stopped dead in his tracks. Two days and he didn't realize he'd left his cell phone, charging, back in his apartment. He had sent her a message that he would be out of town, right? It wouldn't be the first time he wrote a message and then forgotten to hit send. Had he let her know that he'd be out of town for several days? That his brother had died? His heart went to his toes. Would she get a message from Declan if he used his phone? But he didn't remember her number. He had put it into his cell but never *memorized* it. This was not good. He would have missed their dinner that night and the date to spend July 4th with Declan. Did she know Declan's number, to perhaps try to call him to see if something was wrong? No, he doubted she had his phone number, and Al wouldn't have it either. She could call Declan's office though. Then he felt a huge pit in the bottom of his stomach. He had not even told his own company that he was leaving. Would Anna sound an alarm? Maybe he could use Declan's phone and call Anna, then Al and just pass the word? It just seemed like everything kept turning upside down lately. No, he thought, certainly not everything. He had a booming business going. He had found Mariah, and it was getting serious to him. Funerals were always bad additions to any week. He hated them. He hated all this. He'd get a cell phone as fast as he could.

Walking into Defiance Station, it was just as it had always been. But this time he didn't need beer or cigarettes. That was a stunning revelation. He must have shopped in this same store a thousand times and the only thing he had ever bought was cheap beer or cigarettes. He'd have to stroll around and see what else they sold. It would be like a new adventure or something.

"Talon! Long time no see. How are you?"

Talon spotted her at once. She was usually the one working the day shift and she always had a nice word or two for him. Even when he was drunk, she was nice to him. She seemed prettier now, though. Was her hair always that blond? While he doubted there had been any change in her appearance in the near year since he had last been in the store it just seemed like maybe his vision was improved.

"Doing well, Sally. Came up from Virginia to go to Bryce's funeral."

"I'm so sorry, Talon. I didn't know him very well, but he did stop in a couple of times while he was helping your mom get her house repaired."

"He's not suffering anymore, Sally. That's the only good thing."

"I know he was a coal miner, so I'm guessing another death from black lung?"

"Yes. I'm not sure there's a worse way to die – suffocating like that."

"Well, I'm truly sorry, Talon."

Shrugging his shoulders, he heard from behind him, "Oh, My God, Talon!"

Swiftly turning, "Sue? Gosh, HI! How are you?"

This could turn out badly, or maybe not. Sue was probably his most favorite 'lady friend' and she had stayed with him for almost three years. The length of her stay with him was probably the only reason he remembered her name. She was one of the nicer ones. Not so clingy that it made him crazy. She didn't badmouth him either. Or call him names. She still looked good though. Just as he remembered her. He tried to figure out when was the last time he saw her, and he guessed maybe four years ago? He couldn't be sure. His memory of those times wasn't exactly the best for keeping up with timelines.

A little boy ran up to hug his mother's leg. "Hunter, why don't you go pick out *one* toy and I'll get it for you. But only pick out one" Talon looked at the child, cocked his head, then gave Sue a questioning glance.

Hunter disappeared like a bullet shot from a gun. Sue carefully reached up and touched his arm, a small smile barely visible on her lips. "Yes, he's yours, Talon. When I found out I was pregnant with him I had to go into a group home to help me get off the alcohol and drugs and have someone help with what I needed for the baby growing inside me."

Talon just stood there, looking over her shoulder. "I had heard from Molly… well, you know… she was my lover after you, that you had a son that was probably mine. I'm sorry to admit that back then I wasn't exactly 'father' material and didn't really care much about anything. You knew that already, didn't you?"

She drew her lips into a thin line. "Yes. You weren't father material, and you didn't have a cent to your name, so no reason to torture you."

"You didn't want to abort, or give him up for adoption?"

"Trust me. Those thoughts crossed my mind, but in the end, I wanted to have and keep him. My folks were wonderful about it, and it's probably the reason I'm settled and able to raise him to be a good man."

She also said you had married?"

"Yes. I married Ed Granger when Hunter was only a few months old. He's adopted him, Talon, and loves him as much as if he was the biological father. Can you, ah," she shifted her weight from one foot to the other in nervousness, "Can you be alright with that?"

Talon paused, glancing again at the top of his son's head, bouncing up and down the tiny toy section. It tugged at his heart, but he knew he could never meet his needs in any way that would matter. Still…

Shifting his gaze to a back wall, in a thoughtful moment, "I remember Ed. Good man. Always was. Treated me fair. So, yes," Talon paused. "Yes. I'm fine with that. Do you need any help for him? I can pay for some of his growing up. Really, I can."

"No, Ed has a very good job. We have a nice house, and you can see that Hunter is a happy child. I gotta admit, I never in a million years thought I would see you like this. You clean up well, Talon. Seriously. Do you live here?"

"No, I'm down in Virginia now. Declan convinced me to come down there, so I managed to get straight, off the booze, and get a real life. I guess later is better than never, huh?"

"Absolutely. I'm so happy to hear you're finding a new life. You deserve it, Talon. Believe it or not I really care about you. I always have. And," she winked at him, "You're just as handsome as you ever were. What brought you back here? I know your mom and dad both have passed."

"My brother, Bryce, died. Funeral and all, then back to Virginia."

"I'm truly sorry, Talon. I never met him, but it's hard to lose a sibling."

"More than you know," he uttered. "I left my cell phone at home. Would love to have taken a picture of Hunter."

"Give me your number and I'll send you one. Okay?"

Was that a tear forming in the corner of his eye? It would be nice to have a picture, so he quickly turned to ask for a piece of paper and pencil from Sally. Handing the information to Sue, "You have my number now, so if anything happens, or you need help, just call me."

"Thanks, Talon."

"Maybe one more thing," Talon rubbed the back of his neck. "You said Ed adopted him, but for the future, it's alright with me if you ever want to tell him that I'm his biological father. I mean, if he gets curious, or whatever. Kids should be allowed to know all that stuff, I think. He'll always be a Seaton, ya know, just in case...medical stuff and all that..."

Sue smiled, just as Hunter returned. Squeezing Talon's hand, she leaned up and kissed his cheek. "Take care, Talon. And thanks...for everything. What you just said...it's nice to know you don't want to hide."

Leaving with a "catch you later" to Sally, Talon left and started back to the Steele home. He had been told he had a couple of kids. Now he knew one was for sure. Had no clue about any other though and doubted he ever would.

Walking into the kitchen, "Em, could I use your cell for a couple minutes? I forgot mine on the charger, and I need to let Mariah know what's going on here."

Reaching in her purse she handed her phone over to Talon.

"Oh, rats! I keep forgetting I don't know her number. My brain is a sieve."

"Can you call her at work?"

Using the Google app Talon entered Devon Construction, Suffolk, VA, and got a number. Tapping it into her phone, it was answered on the third ring by a breathless voice, "Devon Construction."

"Is Mariah there, please?"

"Naw, she's out somewhere."

Was that noise coming from this woman's mouth, cracking gum, for god's sake? Snap, snap, snap... making his skin crawl.

"Do you know when she's expected back."

"Naw."

"Will you take a message?"

"Yeah."

"Just tell her Talon called and I'm in Pennsylvania at my brother's funeral, and I'll be home Sunday."

"Yeah, sure, I'll do that," and she hung up the phone.

Taking the phone from his ear he stared at it as if he couldn't believe what happened. Making a second call to his office he assured Anna he was fine and the reason for his disappearance. She breathed a sigh of relief. "We were about to call the cops that you were missing." He promised to be back to work Monday. Telling Em what happened, he handed back the phone and asked her not to delete the numbers in her phone log. He had a funny feeling he might need that information again.

Entering the room Declan saw the look on Talon's face. "Everything alright?"

"Hard to tell. I have a sinking feeling Mariah won't get the message I left for her."

The service and funeral for Bryce was well done. Madison seemed to be holding up well, and Talon figured that was because she had seen him suffering so horribly the last year of his life. Her children assured them that they would absolutely see to it that their mom was well taken care of. It was also clear that they meant it. While they didn't know very many of the people at the gathering, Braedon, Talon and Declan stayed to the end. Even Em attended, knowing that Cailen would be well taken care of in her absence.

Paula had set up a small bar-b-que in her backyard. It was a thoughtful gesture to help everyone gather, once again, and begin to heal. Talon and Declan spent some time with Braedon, who had only been able to come up for the one day and was heading back to Washington as soon as he had a brief time with Bryce's family and his brothers.

Talon was just anxious to get home. He was nervous and jittery, and worried about Mariah. Waiting until tomorrow, to head back, was driving him crazy. All he could do was pray everything was alright in Virginia!

The trip back was quiet. Even Cailen slept most of the way with Em forecasting a bad night for her since Cailen would probably be googling and cooing while shifting around in his crib all night long. She foresaw she'd be getting up and walking across the hall to rock him. But she wouldn't trade it for the world. She swore she was going to see if someone made electric rocking chairs for new moms. Push a button and rock. Maybe even a combination lounger/rocker so she could lean back with her feet up. It needed to get invented if it wasn't already on the market. Maybe she'd ask Declan about something like that since he liked making medical equipment. Perhaps it could count as having some form of medical use!

Driving back from Declan's home Talon raced into his apartment and grabbed his cell phone. Quickly hitting Mariah in his favorite's list, all he got was a message that her calls were being forwarded to voice mail. She must have turned her phone off for some reason, even though it wasn't that late at night. Leaving a voice mail about wanting to see her for dinner the next night, he jumped into the shower and then went to bed. It was later than they expected to arrive, and he needed to get up early and make sure there were no problems at the shop. He hadn't bothered to call them, after that one call, trusting that all was well. And, he didn't have any voice mail messages from them, or any phone calls showing in his log. That bothered him and made him open his eyes and wonder why he hadn't seen even one attempt from Mariah to call him. Grabbing his phone off the side table he almost went into shock. He had been in such a hurry getting out of there to go to Pennsylvania that he had *written* her a *text* message, but he had never *sent it to her*. He should have checked his *MESSAGES* the second he got into his apartment. His mind was getting to be mush!

Sitting up in bed, with his legs hanging over the edge, he tried to call Mariah again. Even though it was late at night the call was still going to voicemail after just one ring. He knew what that meant, probably. She had blocked him. Trying to call her again, it was the same one ring and again to voicemail. There was no point in sending a text message now. She would never get it if she had really blocked him. Cripes – he didn't know how all this cell phone stuff worked anyway. Blocking, and forwarding, and letting things go to voicemail. What any ten-year-old could do in a second took him hours to figure out. Like trying to figure out how to turn on the flashlight on the damn thing. He had to ask a 17-year-old store clerk how to do that once. Now his only recourse was to try to catch her as she left work or go to her home and see what happened when she opened the door.

He seriously doubted he had gotten more than 15 minutes of sleep that night but was determined to see Mariah. He was sitting outside her house, early the next morning, just out of view, when she came out and began to back out of her driveway. Quickly moving forward, he blocked her exit. He saw her look in the rearview mirror, so he walked up to her window. Tapping on it, "What's going on, Mariah? I sent you iPhone messages. I left a message for you at your office. What?"

Finally, she opened her car door and stepped out. "Talon," she began, crossing her arms in front of her and making sure he didn't get too close, "I never got a single message from you. Nope. Just leave me hanging for dinner Wednesday night. Not one peep. You weren't at work anymore and my call went to voice mail, which I refused to leave a message. So, you can just stick it, Talon."

"What happened to your face? My GOD, Mariah..."

"I fell. None of your business."

"That's more than a fall, Mariah. I want to know who did this to you." Touching her arm, she quickly retreated from his contact, slapping his hand with hers, as if it were a cattle prod.

"Mariah, please! Talk to me. I swear it's all a misunderstanding. I can explain, honestly."

"Move it, Talon, I swear I will plow right through your car if I have to."

Quickly getting back in her car, she wound down the window just enough to tell him to either get out of her way or she would call the police.

"Mariah. I did leave messages, I have *proof*. My brother died..."

But she had backed up until her rear bumper was just half an inch from the side of his truck. Seeing that she was now making a cell phone call he got back into his truck and pulled it forward to give her enough room to leave. Getting out of his truck he stood there, staring at her, his arms raised in a plea. Turning he watched her car disappear around a corner. What did that remind him of? Crap. Him leaving her standing in the middle of the Lowe's parking lot. Only difference this time was it wasn't raining.

This could not be happening. Why was she being so unreasonable? She didn't even give him a chance. Instead she had likely blocked him from her phone and now had basically told him to go to hell. Pulling into his shop he parked and sat for a minute, running his hand through his hair and trying to understand from her point of view. He was only gone 4 days. And who was the witch that answered the phone at Al's – the one cracking her gum? An *IDIOT*, that's who. There had to be another reason for this to escalate as far as it had. He had worked so hard, for so long, to get back into a normal human mode and now he couldn't help but wonder why he went through it all. For nothing? The only way to keep from hyperventilating was go get out of the car and get back on the job. He'd deal with it later.

Work was agonizing. He was barely able to function. Thankfully his crew and Anna all assumed he was just grieving and didn't ask him any unnecessary questions.

Talon threw himself into his work, hoping that maybe Mariah had heard a sentence or two and would call him. For the next two days he called her, but every attempt went to voice mail. He had to give it up until he could find time to confront her, either at her job or at her home.

Thursday, toward the end of the day, in desperation, he called Al, at Devon.

"Al, I need your help. Mariah has completely misunderstood what happened the four days I was gone, and she won't even let me tell her. It's just an awful series of events that has a good explanation, but she won't let me even begin to tell her. She's probably blocked me from her phone and she almost called the cops on me Monday morning. All I wanted to do was let her give me one minute of her time to know what happened. My brother died. I forgot my cell phone. I was in Pennsylvania. And GOD, what happened to her *face*? I'll kill whoever did that to her…"

"Talon. Oh, Geeze." Lowering his voice, "I'm truly sorry to hear about your brother. First let me tell you that what

I have to say *in no way* affects our business dealings. Second, I believe you. Third, she made me *promise* that if you called me, I was not to tell you anything. She said if I mentioned your name she would quit. I have no idea what's going on in her head regarding you. I would have thought she would be glad to have you back for support."

"Support for what?"

"Ah…" Al paused, aware that he might be saying too much, "Someone to talk to."

"What's with the face lacerations and bruising? It's horrible. What happened to her?"

"Talon, you just have to ask her. I am sworn to silence."

Talon blew out a breath. "Can you tell me who was answering the phones at your office, she chews gum and cracks it constantly?"

"Yes, she's one of our mail room workers, why?"

"Because I called, and she answered, and I left a message for Mariah that obviously was not delivered. You might want to ask her about it, just to set, and keep the record straight."

"I will do just that, Talon. I promise."

Talon could feel his heart empty out. Speaking softly, "Thanks, Al. It doesn't make sense. It just doesn't make sense." He hung up the phone.

One last hope was to go to their favorite pub and see if she showed up.

She didn't.

Back at his apartment, TV blaring and just sitting in his chair, he was lost. When his phone rang, he grabbed it instantly, hoping, but no…

"Hi Declan. You guys alright?"

"Sure. Just thought you'd like to know they finished up the observatory today. It's totally awesome. I can't wait to try it out tonight. Why don't you grab Mariah and come on over and see it?"

"I can come, but Mariah is otherwise busy."

"Is everything alright?"

"Yeah, sure. I'll head on over."

Leaving the television blaring and all the lights on, Talon jumped in his car and headed over to Declan's.

Arriving, Emily immediately noticed the change in Talon's demeanor. "You look down and depressed, Talon. Is everything alright with the business?"

"Never better."

"Mariah is busy tonight?"

"Yup. So, it's dark. Can we go look at the stars?"

"Talon, something isn't right with you."

"I'm fine, Em, just a bit tired, and it was a long day at work, still trying to catch up from being gone." Glancing at her he could tell, without a doubt, that she didn't believe him, but had decided not to press him about it.

"Declan's out at the observatory. Shall we follow?"

Talon reached out and took Cailen from her arms. As they walked, he was grateful that Emily didn't ask any more questions or make any statements about his demeanor. When they finally walked into the observatory, Talon had to admit it was an amazing set-up.

Declan was the epitome of a boy with a new toy. He was practically jumping up and down with excitement. "I think Jupiter is supposed to be up there, but I'm going to have to get some sky charts for the various northern hemisphere seasons, so we can try to figure out what we're looking at. This building is big enough for a few cork boards. This is going to be a lot of fun. Managed to get a bathroom here…had to use one with a septic tank, but that's fine. No shower. Just commode and sink. Water line wasn't too bad. Well, the engineers worked it all out. Even room for a small single bed if someone is here all night. I'll have to put a bed in here, yes. One that is easily moved so you can lie down on it and see the stars through the telescope."

Talon looked at Emily and could almost predict the very reaction she had to that pronouncement!

"NO," Emily pointed to Declan. "No. You are *not* going to spend all night out here. There will be a curfew! Two hours after sunset."

Declan just turned and gave his wife a kiss on the cheek. "Have no fear. You will *never* get rid of me. You're my own personal star."

"A little sappy, but I love it," Em winked at Declan.

Talon felt like he was interrupting something, but needed to get out of the entire situation, "You'll have a really sweet set-up, Declan once you get all the accessories in here. I can't wait until Cailen is old enough to know what he's seeing. I'll try to get back in the next week or so. I need to do some catch-up at work." Well, it was just a tiny lie wasn't it? He was just not up to telling them what was really happening to his emotions. He knew he was starting to spiral out of control but needed a firm grip to continue to stay steady. He was becoming consumed with thoughts about Mariah and what was happening to her. Had a previous boyfriend suddenly shown up and beat her? Had she been in an automobile accident? Those bruises and cuts did *not* come from any fall. It was making him crazy.

Patting Talon on the back, "Sounds like a plan. Let me know when you have time. We will share and share alike, so hopefully Mariah will be able to come back soon too."

Driving home Talon couldn't resist driving past Mariah's to see if she was home. Stopping where he couldn't be seen he watched in shock as a man approached her door, knocked on it, and she let him in, without hesitation. Talon hadn't felt that alone in almost a year. And he had no idea how to deal with it. Well, there was one way…

Three o'clock in the morning. Everything was blurry. So many things going on in his mind. First, he had to figure out where he had ended up. Those flashing lights didn't help his vision. They hurt. He squinted to get a better focus. *Tavern? Bar? Budweiser?* It was a struggle to walk to his car, tripping on a raised bit of concrete walkway, but he managed to open the door and get into it. After fumbling through each of his pockets he managed to find the keys to get it started. Unable to figure out how to clasp his seatbelt, he just threw it back and put the car in gear. Hoping the night air would clear his head he put the driver's side window down and tried sticking his head out the window as he drove. *Drive slowly, Talon. Verrrry slowly. Watch out for any signs of the police.* It took him a few streets to figure out where he was headed. He really hadn't had time to learn the local geography, so street names didn't mean much to him, but he kept driving, slowly, around and around, left then right, until he started to recognize buildings. Housing area. Homes. He had managed, probably subconsciously, to end up in front of Mariah's. Pulling in front of her house, he saw a light shining through the drapery in her front window. Turning off his headlights and placing his car in park he shook his head to try to remember what he was trying to remember! Three o'clock in the morning and a light was on? He wished he could recall the kind of car that guy was driving to see if it was still parked here somewhere, but his fuzzy brain was barely operational. Picking up the bottle of bourbon he had in the seat beside him he drank until he couldn't make any more go down his throat. Stumbling out of the car, bourbon in hand, leaving the door open and keys in the ignition, he realized he hadn't shut the car off. Stumbling back, he reached in and turned it off, but left the keys in the ignition. Once again, he dragged his feet until he reached her door. Ringing the bell, he waited. No response. He rang the bell again. No reply. He tried to call out to her, but his voice wasn't working very well. Then he started ringing the doorbell repeatedly. Finally, he started banging on it with both fists, as hard as he could. Holding up the bottle and practically inhaling the liquor, he stumbled backward, nearly falling off the steps. Twirling and floundering, his eyes began looking up and he felt them rolling back into his head, just as he felt two sets of arms catch him. Suddenly he was on the ground, and then there was nothing.

Mariah saw the police as she pulled back the curtain from the front window. Slowly she opened the door and peered out to see if they had caught the intruder.

Startled as he saw her face, one of the officers approached her. "Did this guy just beat you up, Miss Rogers?" His partner was pulling out handcuffs and was about to put them on Talon's wrists.

Moving closer to the man on the ground she was stunned. "OH, dear GOD, no. Officer that's my boyfriend. Oh, my God, what's the matter with him?" She walked over to where Talon was laying on the ground.

"To say he is drunk is an understatement," said the second officer. Kneeling down to him Andy suddenly expressed concern. "Mark, call rescue. This guy isn't breathing."

"WHAT?" screamed Mariah. "NO, NO. OH, what have I *DONE*?"

Mark immediately called for an ambulance while Andy raced to grab a face mask. Returning he gave a breath, then checked for a pulse. "No pulse," Andy yelled to his partner, quickly beginning chest compressions. Mark returned with the Automated Exterior Defibrillator, attaching it to Talon, then took over compressions as he told his partner the AED said no shock, but the ambulance was on the way.

"NO, OH NO, dear God, NO!" Kneeling down behind the officers she could only watch as they continued to try to keep Talon alive. Foam began drooling from his mouth and they were shaking their heads 'no' just as rescue arrived.

"Whatcha got, Mark?"

"I think he's dead, but for sure," he said, picking up the empty liquor bottle, "he's had a ton of booze down his throat in the last few hours."

Mariah, rocking back on her heels, sat down on the wet, dewy grass, and watched in shock. Rescue was frantically trying to determine if Talon had a pulse. She could barely understand what they were saying as they talked to the doctors at the hospital. Starting an IV, "He is still alive, but just barely. We'll be there in about 11 minutes."

Quickly loading Talon onto a stretcher and into the ambulance, they drove off red light and siren for the hospital.

Still, Mariah hadn't moved. Her skirt and legs were wet, but she didn't feel it. Her shock was evident.

Helping her to her feet, "Miss Rogers, are you okay?"

She could only stare at the officers helping her.

"Did that man beat you up like this?"

Staring back at the officer, she shook her head no.

"Are you sure? You look really badly beat up, ma'am."

Mariah didn't answer.

"Maybe we need to get her to the hospital too."

Grabbing the officer's hand, she stared up at him with glazed over eyes, "Declan Seaton. Call Declan Seaton," she repeated. Then she collapsed. "Andy, put her into the squad car. We'll drive her to the hospital."

Quickly closing the door to her house, Mark also closed the door to Talon's car, securing the keys. Andy and Mark headed to the ER, with Mariah unconscious in the back carefully held by Mark.

"Who did she say to call?"

"Declan Seaton." Andy picked up the mike to contact the dispatcher, asking her to call Mr. Declan Seaton and advise him that possibly a member of his family, along with a Mariah Rogers, had been taken to the hospital.

"Anything else?" asked the dispatcher.

"No, just ask him to please respond as quickly as possible."

Chapter 9

Arriving as quickly as he could get there, Declan hurried into the ER and gave his name.

"Yes, Mr. Seaton. I believe they need you down in bay four." Pointing to the direction he should go, Declan turned and hurried to the bay stations. It wasn't hard to miss bay 4. It was where everyone was standing around a gurney while two doctors, and he couldn't count the nurses, were frantically working on someone. Police officers stood toward the back, rescue workers were assisting the nurses… another gurney was right next to it, probably in bay 5, but the curtains had been drawn back. More doctors and nurses. IV's were being strung, but whatever was happening in bay four was obviously considerably more important than the side gurney.

"Intubate," called a doctor. "NOW!"

More flurry.

"Lab just came back, doctor, BAC is 3.5, a nurse called out over the whirlwind of activity."

"Dear Jesus! This guy is one step from dead. One more drink would have done it. Oxygen on," stated the resident.

"Yes, good," said the attending doctor. "We have the IV's in?"

"Yes, doctor."

"With luck, and a lot of help from God, he'll make it. He needs to go to ICU, stat. He needs monitoring overnight." Nurses quickly threw back the curtains to allow for the gurney to be wheeled from the bay.

"Yes, doctor."

Standing back, stunned at what he was watching, he couldn't believe his eyes when the gurney quickly being pushed down the hall, directly in front of him, was occupied by his unconscious brother. A police officer was following closely.

Pushing his back against the wall to allow for ease of passage, he watched until the double doors to the ICU closed. Two doctors came out, and Declan called to them.

"Yes, sir," said one of them. "Are you related?"

"That's my brother you just sent to ICU. What *happened*?"

"Alcohol Poisoning. One more drink and he would not be alive right now."

"Oh, my God. He's been sober for, well, close to a year."

"Can you give his identification information to the nurse, please?" asked one of the doctors.

"Yes, of course. But who is in that other bed?"

"I'll have the police officer talk to you."

Looking toward the other bed Declan was aghast to see Mariah lying there, her face a mess of bruises and cuts. Waiting for the officers he made a quick call to Emily.

"Emily, I don't know what happened yet. Apparently, Talon got so drunk tonight he almost died. They barely saved him. He's in ICU now. Mariah was also brought in at the same time, and she is badly beaten. I don't know any more, but I'll call when I do. I'm waiting to talk to the police officer now." He paused. "Em, please don't cry. He'll live. I just don't know any more right now. I'll call as soon as I get the story straight."

Pushing the CALL STOP button, the officer he was waiting for arrived.

"I'm Andy,"

"Officer, what happened?"

"Well, we aren't exactly sure. We got a call from the lady, ah, Miss Rogers, that someone was ringing her doorbell and knocking on her front door like he was gonna bust it. We arrived just as the guy was falling down drunk off the steps. When we helped lower him to the ground the lady opened the door and she was all busted up. Her face was full of cuts and bruises. One of the doctors in there just said she has a lot of bruising on her total body, but they are older trauma, so it didn't happen tonight. Now, when she came out of the house, she said the guy on the ground was her boyfriend. When rescue arrived, we noticed the lady was rather in a trance, shook her head 'no' when we asked her if the guy rescue was working on had done all that to her. Then as *she* collapsed, she said to call Declan Seaton, and I expect you are him?"

"Yes. The man is my brother Talon, and the lady is Miss Mariah Rogers. She and Talon have been dating. He would never do that to her."

"She did say no, but you have to understand we must be sure of it before we leave him unguarded. My partner is checking police records to see if we have any reports of an assault on Miss Rogers."

"Yes. Good. I need to call her uncle. He'll be a basket case."

Knowing now that Al would likely be at work by then, he input the phone number, and when Al answered he gave him all the information.

"Oh, Cripes! Can we not catch any breaks in all this drama?"

"I know Talon hasn't been able to get Mariah to talk to him. But he would never abuse her or hurt her in any way."

"No, it wasn't Talon. But his leaving without telling her set it all up."

"What does that mean? I don't understand," questioned Declan

"Mariah will have to explain, Declan. Just know that she blames Talon for abandoning her at the diner."

Declan could tell by the tone of his voice that Al was getting angry about Talon doing stuff that abused his niece.

"I understand, Al. Honest I do, but there has to be reasons for all of this. If these two would just talk to each other then maybe... *maybe*... all these misunderstandings... I'm as frustrated as you are, Al."

"Yeah, I get it, Declan. I apologize for my outburst. I'll be there as soon as someone gets here to cover the office."

Calling Emily again he brought her up to speed. "I don't think Talon beat her up, Emily, but something is going on with that. I need to find out what, so I can deal with Talon drinking again. Just try to relax, hon. I'll stay here." Finally, calling his office he let Laura know what was going on. He was glad to hear he did not have any appointments scheduled for the day.

It was only about twenty minutes before Al arrived and managed to find Declan in the ICU. Motioning for him to come into the hall for a few minutes, and shaking his hand, "Hi, Declan. I'm sorry to meet you under these circumstances. But I need to fill you in, and the officer too, if he'll come forward."

Declan beckoned for the officer to join them.

"Okay, Mariah swore me to secrecy, but this is beyond any need for that," began Al. Shuffling his feet, "Declan, the night that all of you apparently left for your brother's funeral,

Mariah went to the pub to meet Talon, as prearranged, and their usual habit. But your brother never showed, so after two hours she decided to go home. As she left a man came out of the pub behind her and made a pass at her. Refusing him, he suddenly grabbed her, dragged her into the bushes on the side of the property and was beating her in the face. He took out a knife and made a couple of marks on her face, to draw blood, and then started to cut off her clothing. She was screaming but the band noise in the bar was louder than her screams. Just then two people drove up and the only place to park was close to those bushes. They heard Mariah screaming and rushed to see what the problem was. The attacker jumped up, pointed his knife at the two witnesses, and then ran off. The couple immediately called for police and rescue, and Mariah spent the next three days in the hospital."

"OH. MY. GOD." Whispered Declan. "And the worst part is we didn't leave for Pennsylvania until the next morning. I have no idea why Talon didn't meet her for dinner unless his brain just left his body for some stupid reason. I can't believe he just forgot about Mariah, even under those circumstances. He had plenty of time to eat dinner with her then get home and pack and get a good night's sleep before the trip. It just doesn't make sense."

"I now know," continued Al, "That Talon thought he sent her a message, but he never hit the send button, and, in the rush to get to your brother's funeral he forgot his phone. Talon tried to call her once, from what he said, from Pennsylvania, but she never got that either, or she refused to open the voice mail. Or she was still in the hospital recovering. I don't know. Talon also called the office and left a message for her and I will deal with the employee who did not give it to her, or at least mention it to me. Mariah was in the hospital at that time. I would have gladly delivered the message to her."

"Did they get the guy that beat her up?"

Both looked at the police officer, who had been smart enough to be taking notes. "I don't know about that case, but my partner is checking police records now. Regardless there's no reason for me to stay and watch, ah, Talon, since he is not the guy that beat her up."

As the officer left to see what he could find out, "Declan, there's a bit more."

"Go ahead."

"Mariah is blaming Talon. She is a bit twisted right now, and not thinking straight, but she feels that because Talon stood her up, she sat there longer than normal waiting for him, which gave that guy more time to watch her. She's *terrified* now, and that's normal. I think after this maybe both of them need some heavy-duty therapy. Maybe even together!"

"How can stuff get so messed up in such a short time?"

"Declan, when you find the answer, let me know. I'm going to go back to Mariah now and see what can be done. Maybe this incident will help in the long run. Who knows?"

"Thanks, Al. Please keep me posted." Taking a card out of his pocket he wrote something on it, "My personal cell number."

Giving Declan his own, "Thanks, and let me know how Talon does, please."

A few minutes later the officer came back to tell them that the guy hadn't been caught, but everyone at the pub was on the lookout should he ever come back. Walking out with Declan they again saw Al and passed the information on to him. As the officer left, Al let Declan know that they were going to keep Mariah a couple of days to be sure she was stable. She was still in a state of shock and not speaking but seemed to be improving slowly.

"Al, a thought. What if we ask the hospital to put Declan and Mariah in the same room – or if nothing else both of us getting together and putting them in counseling together. They need to *talk to each other*. If they can't do that then all is lost, I fear. I've never seen Talon adore anything or anyone like he does Mariah. He got drunk because he doesn't understand. She's lashing out because *she* doesn't understand."

"Good thinking."

"In fact, they can use my home. It has an entire separate wing, and I can have the best psychiatrist in the area come to see them privately, if necessary. I have a personal home chef, so all expenses on me. They might not even need a psychiatrist if they would just listen to each other. That can be arranged easily enough at my home."

"Oh, I like that maybe they can rediscover their feeling for each other. Also, they can have the solitude with family around, and hopefully you'll allow me to visit."

"You're a family member now. If we can get this set up, you'll have the gate code."

Parting ways with Al going toward Mariah and Declan toward the ICU, he agonized over what Talon was going to have to go through, all over again. And worse, Declan suspected, if Mariah rejected him it could well end in disaster.

Chapter 10

Emily was sitting at the kitchen table, feeding Cailen, as Declan walked into the kitchen. Looking up at him, "Talon?"

With a sigh, Declan sat down. "Is he alright?" begged Emily, "I mean… he isn't…"

"No, he is stable. They have him in ICU overnight. Mariah too, overnight, but not in ICU."

Watching a tear roll down his wife's cheek, Declan explained everything he knew about the situation, including how Mariah had been assaulted.

Reaching down to gently wipe the tear from her eye, "I hate to say it, Emily, but it seems to me that it's just completely impossible for communication links to break down like they did between those two, until I think about how close we came to disaster because of the very same thing."

Emily was silent. Wiping Cailen's mouth she got up and put him in his little swing. "Prognosis?"

"Time will tell, Emily, but I've offered the East Wing of our home to Mariah and Talon so that maybe we can get some psychiatric help in for both, individually and/or together. It might be all they need. Or maybe all they need is just space and time to talk and listen to each other. Al is all for his niece staying here for that reason." Taking Emily's hand, "What are your thoughts? Is all that okay with you? I can change it all in a minute!"

"We'll do whatever it takes to get them both well again."

"Are you sure? You seem detached somehow?"

"I guess I am just worried sick about Talon. And I'm disappointed that he didn't say anything when he was in the observatory with us. It could have been *so* different if he had shared his feelings. Maybe we could have talked to Mariah and let her know what happened with Bryce and the phone mess-up. He *did* try to call her. I was sitting right there, but then he couldn't remember her phone number. It's one of the reasons cell phones are not helpful – when you don't have them. Not to mention you can't get a phone number for a cell from anyone but the owner! So, he called her at work and some dippy woman answered. Apparently, the dip didn't leave the message for Mariah. I guess it's the entire sequence of events that is making me a bit angry, and more because Talon didn't share his pain with us – that's the worst of it. He could have *said* something."

"Yes. And knowing the chain of events, Mariah had already been assaulted. Maybe that's why some dip answered the phone at Al's! Mariah was in the hospital recovering from the assault!" Declan put his finger to his temple. "Now it's beginning to make sense. She's home, scared, wounded, and someone starts banging on her door and ringing the doorbell at three in the morning. And down everyone goes. Well. Maybe that's what it takes to solve this."

"Declan, you know I'll do anything I can to help." Stopping to watch her son swinging, she looked back at Declan. "Look what we have. I am so blessed to have both of you. I've loved you for so long, Declan. I'm almost able to understand what happened to Talon when Mariah rejected him. I know I shed enough tears over you."

Reaching down to pick her up from the chair, Declan kissed her with passion. "You. Are. My. Everything." Letting her go after a strong hug, Emily could see tears forming in his eyes. Giving him a quick peck on the cheek, "You go set everything up and I'll start on the East Wing!" Picking up Cailen and putting him in his stroller, "Let's go have fun getting the East Wing ready, kiddo!"

"I'll hire more help. Cleaning and all. A weekend Chef, whatever we need. You just let me know."

Emily couldn't help but smile, despite the seriousness of the situation. Declan had declared, when she promised to marry him, that he would always take care of Talon, regardless, and he was keeping that promise. It gave her a warm feeling in her heart to see him care so much for the brother who had made his life a living hell when they were children.

At breakfast the next morning Declan called the hospital. "They said Talon might be moved as early as eleven this morning, so I'll check in with work and then go back to the hospital. Do you want to call someone in to watch Cailen and then come with me?"

"You go ahead. I'll stay here in case any new housekeepers or chefs show up. I know how fast you work, dear-heart."

He smiled. No one would ever understand how much he loved that woman.

"Mr. Seaton, your brother is now in room 208."

"What about Mariah Rogers?"

"She's in the next room, 210."

Walking into Talon's room he had no idea what to expect. But Talon was awake, and the tube had been removed from his throat. He was no longer on oxygen. But he was lying there, staring up at the ceiling, both hands grasping the bed sheet as if he was afraid he would fall if he let loose.

"Talon?"

Talon's eyes shifted toward the sound, and Declan saw tears streaming down his face. Carefully reaching down Declan wiped them with his index finger and thumb. Pulling up a chair he removed a tissue from the box and continued to wipe tears, as they fell. "Can you look at me, Talon?"

As Declan carefully unclutched Talon's hand from the sheet, then held it, Talon slowly turned his head and recognized Declan.

"Talk to me brother."

He stared at his brother for a few moments, letting out a sigh and grasping Declan's hand. "I am so sorry, Declan. I just went nuts. She let a guy into her house and I just went crazy. She doesn't answer any of my calls, or texts, or emails. Nothing." Almost choking out words, "I just don't know what I did that was so wrong," tears began to fall freely.

"We'll figure it all out, Talon. Honestly." He continued to wipe the tears from his brother's face.

Shifting a bit in his bed, "Mariah?" he questioned.

"She's in the next room. I need to explain some things to you. Al is also in her room talking to her. She's in bad shape, Talon."

"Why?"

Talon listened as Declan explained what had happened to Mariah.

"Oh, dear, God," moaned Talon. "Oh, no. Did he?"

"NO! Talon. The witnesses got to her before he could cut all her clothes off."

"Have they found him?"

"No, but they will. I won't let them rest until they do."

"She blames me because I wasn't there?" Talon turned his head away and took a deep breath to keep from sobbing.

"For the moment. That will change. One thing for sure, though, we don't understand why you didn't have dinner with her regardless. There was plenty of time."

"I guess I was so stunned by Bryce's death I wasn't thinking. Crap, I even forgot to *send* the message I wrote to her. Then I forgot to take my own phone with me to Defiance. All I could think of was that I didn't want to go back there, for any reason, yet I had to go back for Bryce."

Declan nodded, understanding. "How are you doing right now?"

"I feel like crap – the booze – why did I do that? I need to get ahold of myself. She made me nuts, and now…now I don't know. I have to wonder if it's all worth it. All the BS. All the trust issues. She wouldn't even give me a *chance* to explain, and that's just not fair. I hope she'll be alright, but I don't see how we can get past this. Anyway, she's eleven years younger than me. Maybe it's just too many years. It all just hurts too much."

"Would you be willing to work with her, in counseling, staying in the East Wing, for a couple weeks? I have a psychiatrist on stand-by to help both of you, *if* needed, but right now I think she needs a lot more help than you do. Maybe you can support her gently and help her get past this attack."

"Right now, I don't think anything will help. I feel like I just walked through hell again, and it's not worth the price I paid. You tell me what to do and I'll try to do it. I know Aaron, Jacob and Anna can keep the place running just fine until I get back, but I don't think I'll be gone all that long for them to worry about any of it."

"I'll take care of it. So, let's take baby-steps. Don't try to see Mariah just yet. Let us arrange it to *her* satisfaction. You might scare her again, like you did last night, and then she'll refuse all attempts to help her. Can you agree to that?"

"Sure. Why not? She's done a stellar job of ignoring me so far, so there's no point in pushing my way into her life again. One 'no' out of her mouth and I'm total history. Can we agree on *that,* Declan?"

Declan nodded his head yes, but it was clear he wasn't happy about it. "Talon, I don't want to add to your desolation, but I need to let you know that both Emily and I are disappointed that you didn't trust us enough to share your feelings when you came to see the observatory. We could have taken steps right then to help you."

"God, Declan. I know. It was selfish of me to hold back. I could see Em didn't believe me when I said I was fine, but I just couldn't bring myself... I mean... I didn't know what was happening, or why Mariah was avoiding me. I just felt so awful, worrying that someone else had come back into her life, or that she might have found someone new in the short time I was gone... and that guy I saw her let into her house earlier that night... I'm so very sorry. It won't happen again. I promise you I'll talk to you guys if I ever feel the need to walk into a bar ever again."

Declan patted Talon on the shoulder. "You rest now. I'll check and see when you can be released, and Al and I will work together on this. Can I trust you, Talon? You do know you almost died last night, don't you?"

"Yes, I know." Talon looked toward Declan, finally locking eyes. "The doctor was in here first thing this morning. He told me I had one foot in the grave. I guess I should be thankful that Mariah called the police. If I had given up and gone back to the car, I probably would be dead." He closed his eyes for a moment. Opening them, "And yes. You can trust me. I have no desire to mess anything else up."

"I'll be back."

"Tell Em I'm recovering. Just one night off the wagon is all."

"I'll tell her. She's mighty worried."

"Let's work toward a sober party at that telescope. Just the four of us."

"Good thinking, Talon. I'll check on you later."

Declan had a busy day to deal with. Hire more help for the house. Find a new chef for the weekends. Talk to the psychiatrist. Get the East Wing ready – well, he knew Emily was on that already, just in case Al and Mariah agreed. He also wanted to check with the police to see what progress had been made as well as speak to the officers who had responded to the assault case. He wanted to know if they thought the man might have Mariah's address. If so, Mariah would be moved to a much safer, permanent location, with intense security. He would see to all of it. Whatever was needed.

Declan had only been gone about 10 minutes when Al came into the room. "Hi, Talon. How do you feel? It's nice to see that they don't have you hooked up to so much stuff anymore."

"I've been better, but at least I'm alive. Mariah?"

"She's awake now. She's asking if she can see you? You rather scared the hell out of her last night when she realized…"

It was like a spark going through his body. "Yes, she can see me. I mean, if she really wants to. I'll get up…"

"No, I'll bring her in here in a wheelchair. If it starts out well, I'll go get a cup of coffee so you two can talk a bit, if that's alright with you."

Knowing it would take a few minutes to get Mariah out of her bed and into a wheelchair was going to be hard. He started checking out every little detail of the room to keep his mind busy – the TV that was turned off, small, but well located high on the wall across from his bed. A small cabinet where he figured his clothes were, if anything was left of them. Probably had to cut them off him. A comfortable chair. An open door, obviously leading to the bathroom. Even a window to look out of, with nothing but trees to see. So, he started counting trees, from left to right…

Talon had never been so nervous in his entire life. He was shaking as the wheelchair began to come through the door. Al rolled her up near to Talon.

Turning to see her face, "Oh, my GOD, Mariah." Looking at her face and arms he was shocked at how badly beaten she had been. "I didn't see all that when I came over that morning." Tears poured from his eyes in his absolute shock at the bruising and cuts. Putting his hands over his eyes, he sobbed.

Taking his hand away and gently turning his head, she took a tissue and began wiping away his tears, then used the same tissue to wipe away her tears that had formed watching him suffer so much.

Finally, able to speak, "I had a lot of heavy makeup over most of it. You couldn't have seen it all. Plus, the bruise colors get darker before they get lighter."

"Were there any broken bones? I am so sorry, and it was all my fault. I should have called you when we got the word… Bryce…" tears started streaming down his face again. He felt weaker and weaker as he tried to explain what had happened to her. His emotions were totally out of control at this point.

Reaching over she took Talon's hand. "No, no broken bones. It's over, Talon. We have both suffered and all because of misunderstandings and miscommunications. Neither of us had any way of knowing…"

She watched as Talon took his free hand and covered his eyes again. "What that guy did to you…"

"Shhh, Talon." Turning and motioning to Al, she gestured that it was fine if he went for that cup of coffee, so he silently walked out of the room. Moving her wheelchair closer and putting on the brakes, she stood up and sat on his bed, waiting for him to look at her again. "Talon, I'm here for you. Yes, I was hurt, badly, and I felt abandoned… and I missed you so much and didn't know why you would have stood me up."

"I tried to contact you…I…"

"Shh," she put her finger to his lips. "Al explained what happened. Some of it anyway. Enough that I know you didn't intentionally abandon me like that."

Slowly turning toward her he lifted his hand from his eyes, squinting as he took her hand. "Oh, Mariah, you're beautiful. Nothing will ever change that. But there is so much about me you don't know. It scares me."

"Al told me that we might be able to deal with some of our 'issues' at Declan's. Communication. Trust. Are you willing to try that for two weeks? Al said I can have the time off. I don't know about your business."

"Aaron and Jacob can handle most anything. I can be available through cell, and we both know Al is my biggest client. He certainly understands…"

"Do you want to try? Talon, he told me about your brother dying and how you tried to send me a message and then forgot to hit the send button. He said you left a message at the office for me, but I never got it. I'm not sure it would have mattered then because I was so sore and hurting from the beating. Maybe at that time nothing would have worked. When I saw you on the ground and they were saying you had died, I…

"Oh, Mariah. Yes. I'll do anything," he interrupted. All he could do was stare at her, trying to memorize every feature, every line of her face – her jaw, her cheeks, her forehead. Her lovely, clear skin now battered – covered with bruises and cuts. No sutures. Just suture tape. He figured that meant the cuts weren't too terribly deep or there would have been stitches, but he wasn't sure about that. Moving his eyes down to her arms they were just as black and blue from the struggling, grabbing, that monster's vicelike grip. Talon felt he would never be able to make it up to her.

Leaning down she gently rubbed his cheek with her finger, then kissed him gently. She could feel the shiver in his body, and when he opened his eyes there was no doubt in her mind that he was very much in love with her, but there was a fear looming in the background. They had a lot of talking to do.

Taking a deep breath, "Okay, then. We're both being released shortly. I'll see you at Declan's then."

All Talon could do was smile and try to stop his heart from beating so rapidly.

Chapter 11

Emily and her cleaning staff made a complete sweep of the East Wing. Bathrooms were en suite to each bedroom and were now spotless. Each room was dusted and swept, and the queen size beds were redressed with fine sheets and a comforter. Chairs, and dressers were ready. Each room had individual heat/cool settings, and while there was a nook where a coffee pot could be set up, Emily opted to omit that in order to force both of her guests to come to the kitchen for coffee and breakfast.

Leaving the rooms, she was pleased at how lovely they looked. They were large rooms, and each had a fifty-inch television on the wall. Colors were always neutral, throughout the house, making decorating changes easy, but the molding was stained a walnut color and added to the overall beauty of the entire East Wing. There were two other rooms she could have selected, but they were toward the back of the wing, and these two were right across from each other. Solid doors were on each room, as well as at the entrance to the East Wing. Total privacy was assured, yet they were free to roam the house as they wished. Nothing confined them to the East Wing, in any way. She and Declan had discussed that in a phone call when he went to pick up Talon. She hung up as he arrived at the hospital.

Both Talon and Mariah were ready to leave. It was mandatory that staff wheel them to the curb where they were assisted into the Limo. Declan thanked them for their help and got into the seat facing them. Max slowly left the entrance, heading out of the hospital complex.

"Declan," began Talon. "Any chance we could stop by and let me pick up my car? I'm well enough to drive and it would be handy to have it in case I need it for something?"

"Me too," quickly interrupted Mariah.

Declan took a long, hard look at both. Mariah seemed to be the most relaxed of the two, sitting back against the seat, head against the headrest, arms loosely across her stomach, legs comfortably bent in front of her. Talon was wound up like a tightly compressed spring. Sitting forward, hands thumping his knees, tapping one foot and biting his lip. "Max, take Miss Rogers to get her car."

"Address sir?"

Giving Max her address, they all remained silent as Max turned the car to accommodate her request.

"What about *me*, Declan?"

"No, Talon. I don't think so. You might bolt trying to find the guy that hurt Mariah, and I'd rather the police did all that."

"But my car?"

"I have cars. You know that. And Max is available at any time. But for the moment you won't have access to anything but Max."

Sitting back with a *huff,* Talon was not happy, and looked out the window, even as they pulled into Mariah's and she got out and closed the door behind her. Max waited until she was able to pull in behind him, then they continued the drive toward Declan's home.

"*Not fair*, Declan. Why did you let Mariah get her car and not me?"

"Because you are a time bomb waiting to explode. Pulling you out of jail is not on my list of things I want to do tonight, Talon. I want to go home, have dinner and enjoy my wife and son. It's been a long day."

Although Talon didn't say anything, there was no doubt in Declan's mind that he would have to watch him, carefully. In fact, maybe a good talking to, from both Emily and he, might even be in order. He'd talk to Emily about it before dinner, when Talon and Mariah were settling into their rooms.

Emily met them all at the door and escorted Mariah to her room. "Talon, I moved you across the hall from your original room. Mariah might prefer a bathtub, and that's the only bath with one in the East Wing. You have a very nice shower, though."

Without acknowledging her in any way Talon threw his few possessions into the new room assigned to him and closed the door. Mariah merely shrugged her shoulders, with a sigh, and walked into her room. "Gosh, Emily. This is amazing!"

Emily smiled. "We hope you are comfortable. And, by the way, I asked Al to pick up some of your clothing and things he might think you could use. They are in those suitcases, and some clothing has already been hung."

Sitting on the edge of the bed, Mariah could feel tears forming in her eyes, but knew strength was going to be important if she was going to help Talon.

Emily walked over and gave her a hug. "It will be alright, Mariah. This is just day one-half. I'll let you get organized and refreshed and dinner will be in about one hour."

Mariah nodded as Emily left, closing the door behind her.

"Emily, we are going to have to watch Talon. He is seething inside, and not just because I wouldn't let him pick up his car. He's after the guy that hurt Mariah and unless we figure out a way to keep him here, he *will* bolt."

"Yes." Emily stopped to sit down on the family room sofa. "Talon is just an emotional person. Don't get me wrong Declan, he's almost the opposite of you. You rarely show emotion in public, and Talon will toss it all over the yard if he's unhappy. He'll punch out anyone, anytime."

"That's what scares me. His first move will be to go down to the pub and start asking questions about who went out the door after Mariah that night. Everybody there knows both of them, so they'll gladly tell him anything they know. Then he'll make a beeline to find him. If he doesn't kill him, he'll still end up with a felony assault. He could lose everything…" Declan paused, "I need to talk to him, now."

Standing to take Declan's hand, "Yes. I think you do. In the meantime, I'll find a new hiding place for the keys to all the cars. At least that will force Talon to use Max, and he knows Max would never take him to the pub."

"I'll make double sure Max knows he's not to take him anywhere for a day or two and then only if he checks with me first."

"Good. Knowing Talon, he'll tell Max to take him to his apartment, then he'll bolt from there, walking if necessary, to get to that bar."

"No, he'll hitch-hike. That's even worse."

Declan needed to determine his approach as he walked down the East Wing hall. Tapping on Talon's door, and not getting a reply, he tapped again, louder.

"Alright! Come in."

"We need to talk, Talon."

"Talk or lecture."

"Whatever it takes."

Rolling over with his back to Declan, he waited for the tirade.

"Talon, do you honestly and truly love Mariah?"

That question surprised Talon. It took a few moments for him to answer. "Yes."

"Enough that you want her to marry you?"

Another pause – a longer pause, then a barely audible "Yes."

"Do you want to keep your furniture making company?"

"What's with the questions?"

"Do you want to keep your furniture making company?" Declan asked, calmly, evenly and without any edge to his voice.

Talon sighed, "Yes."

"You aren't a prisoner here, Talon. You are a guest. Mariah is a guest. If you bolt, and go after the guy that hurt her, and find him, what do you think will happen."

"I'll kill him."

"Then what, assuming no one catches you that instant and you have to get away?"

No answer.

"What will you do, Talon?"

Waiting for an answer, Declan looked around the room at the lovely pictures Emily had found for the walls. Peaceful, coordinated, nice job.

"I'll head to Pennsylvania as fast as I can?"

"And go back to your shed?"

"Yes."

"And give up Mariah and your business?"

"What do you want from me, Declan?"

"Understanding. Some smart thinking."

"I'll take Mariah with me."

"Do you think she'd like living in a shed?"

No answer.

"So, let's say you get caught by the cops. What do you think will happen?"

"I'll spend the night in jail."

"With a felony assault or a murder charge hanging over your head?"

No answer

"Do you think Mariah, or your business will still be there when you get out of prison?"

"OH, CRAP, DECLAN. STOP MAKING SENSE," exploded Talon, his body stiffening.

"Talon, you need to think all that through. We both know you would never see Mariah again, regardless of which way it went. She loves you. You two *can* work it out and let the police do their job. They'll get him. They know what they're doing. And I'll be on their backs to not drop it. Just think about it. Will you do that please? We'll call when dinner is ready."

Softly closing Talon's door, Declan saw that Mariah's was open and she wasn't there. He found her talking to Emily, in the family room. Both invited him into their conversation.

"Is he okay?" asked Mariah.

"Let's just say I gave him a lot to think about. How he handles those decisions will tell us all we need to know." Gently putting his hand on Emily's shoulder, "I'm starving. When's dinner?"

"Chef just advised us fifteen minutes. Time to wash up. I'll wait five and then ring Talon."

"That should answer our question." Observed Declan. "He'll show up and be civil and repentant, or, he won't show up at all and will try to vanish by morning. I'll activate the electric fencing now, just in case."

He motioned for Emily to help Mariah' who had begun to cry, then walked into the dining room to give them space. Giving them a couple of minutes, he pushed the button to let Talon know dinner was ready.

A chime resounded in Talon's room, the signal that dinner was ready. Sitting on the edge of the bed and watching the birds gather around the bird baths and feeders outside his windows he made his decision.

Putting on his best face he walked into the dining room, leaned down and kissed Mariah on the cheek, then sat down beside her. Taking her hand and squeezing it he was surprised to see tears coming down her cheeks. Leaning over he whispered something in her ear that brought a smile to her face.

Dinner turned out to be relaxed, and Declan breathed a sigh of relief that Talon had been able to come to grips with actions and consequences. He nodded as he saw Talon Give a wink to Emily; she smiled back at him.

"It's good to have you back with us for a bit, Talon. Heck, I might even let you play with Cailen. He should be awake by now."

Jumping up so fast his chair almost fell, "I'll go get him. You just bring on the dessert, Em."

Talon raced out of the room, returning a few minutes later with Cailen. "I even changed his diaper for you."

Mariah gazed up at him, "You do good work, Talon," she smiled. Suddenly Emily could see that their eyes were now dancing more with love, than fear. She watched as Talon sat back down next to Mariah and offered to put Cailen in her arms. She took him eagerly.

Talon was the first to excuse himself to head to the bedroom. He had one change of clothing. He'd have to have Declan, or someone, get him more clothing. Shaking his head, he shouldn't have moved out all his stuff so soon. But he was tired. He had no conversation left tonight. He heard Mariah close the door to her room. He could well imagine she was exhausted as well.

The next six days slowly passed. Talon and Mariah spoke to each other a little more each day. It wasn't easy. He was so afraid she would dump him when, and if, he got the courage to be honest with her. Communication became easier and easier. They could be found sitting near each other on the family room sofa, sometimes watching television, sometimes listening to music, and occasionally holding hands. Emily and Declan made it a point to say absolutely nothing to either of them, regarding their process. General conversation was the order of the day at dinner and other gathering times. Except for giving Declan the key to his apartment and asking that Max pick up some of his clothing, nothing else was said about the ongoing situation. Mariah left once to get more clothing, even though the washer and dryer were available to her. She was only gone an hour, but it was obvious Talon missed her. He paced. But Emily knew better than to ask him why he was pacing. She took Cailen for walks on the grounds, pushing the stroller and sitting under some of the large, beautiful trees that surrounded their home. She thought about offering that suggestion to Talon and Mariah. Might help them to be outdoors. They'd spent the past week pretty much staying indoors of their own choice. They could even go to the observatory if they wanted to look at the stars.

Walking back into the house she noticed that Mariah had returned while she was sitting in the back yard with Cailen. "Gosh, the weather outside is so beautiful. Perfect temperature, slight breeze, sun shining. Doesn't get any better." She continued to walk past Mariah to take Cailen up for his nap.

Glancing out the window after settling Cailen in his bed, she noticed Talon and Mariah, walking hand in hand, down the grass toward the location of the observatory. *Good,* she thought. *They're holding hands. Excellent.* It was like they had read her mind!

They were all pleased when Al called and asked if it would be convenient for him to visit Mariah. Arriving at lunch time he found a place set for him at the table and a lunch that made his stomach growl in anticipation.

"Mariah said you like Reuben sandwiches," said Emily. "All of us do too, and the chef is a master at making them."

As they ate the conversation was light and happy. Mariah was thrilled to see her uncle again and they talked about work and how they needed to get her back there as soon as possible. With lunch finished and Al's comment that it was the best Reuben he had ever eaten, he and Mariah got up.

"You two go ahead and talk," said Talon. I know Al has to get back to work. I'll just get another cup of coffee.

As they left the room Talon was almost positive he heard Al ask Mariah if she had told him yet. And he heard Mariah mumble some form of reply, but he wasn't able to understand it. Curious, he thought. He wondered what Al was alluding to. Tell who what? Sitting in the kitchen he tried to think of any other 'him' Al might be talking about. Maybe her brother? Didn't seem likely he was referring to any of the workers. He'd have to think about it for a while.

Al left a few minutes later and Mariah walked to the East Wing.

"What's going on in that mind of yours Talon? You're too quiet right now."

"Nothing, Em. Just thinking. Wondering why Mariah went to her room, I guess."

Noticing the distant look in Talon's eyes, "I noticed the two of you walking down toward the observatory, earlier."

"Hmm," he turned toward Emily. "Yes. We walked down that way but not into the observatory. I think I'll go take a nap."

"I'll see you later then."

Dinner that night was one of the chef's specialties. When Emily told him she wanted a special dinner that night he was more than happy to serve up his special meal – steak, with his own sauce recipe, potatoes that only he knew the secret recipe for, and a good vegetable. Dessert would be his special chocolate mousse. No one could resist his chocolate mousse.

Emily had been right. Not one speck of food was left on any of the four plates.

"Amazing dinner, Emily. My compliments to the chef," said Talon. "Loved every bite."

"He'll be happy to know it. I told him I thought tonight might be a bit special. You and Mariah have done so well, over the past week, that I wanted to have a special meal."

Declan smiled at his wife, then cleared his throat.

"Both Emily and I feel you two have progressed to the point that you can continue your lives in your own places." began Declan. "Of course, you are welcome to stay here as long as you feel the need. Or return at any time. We love both of you."

Emily nodded in agreement and watched as both Talon and Mariah smiled at each other.

"Alright," Declan started, "Emily will feed Cailen so why don't you two go down and see the observatory. Mariah hasn't seen it yet, Talon, and you can show her what's been done."

"YES!" breathed Mariah. "I would love it."

Turning on the overhead door that opened to the night sky, they adjusted everything, and Mariah put her eye to the scope.

"Oh, my word," marveled Mariah. "I have never seen anything this beautiful. Oh, Talon, this is amazing. Totally amazing. I can watch through the telescope or set it to show on the monitor."

Choosing to look through the telescope, Mariah continued, "Do you know how far away our nearest star neighbor is?"

"Nope."

"Well, Proxima Centauri is 4.24 light years away. So, let's assume you are standing above the Milky Way Galaxy, then you zoom way in and pick one tiny star between the edge and middle of the outer arm of the galaxy. Let's say that's our sun. Now pick the star right next to it. Zoom out to see the entire galaxy. Huge. Almost impossible to find those two stars again. But those stars are 4.24 light years apart. Got that so far?"

She could see him trying to draw some kind of map in his head to understand what she way describing.

"I think so."

To travel to our nearest neighbor, Proxima Centauri, would take over 80 thousand years. Eighty THOUSAND years!!! So, how long do you think it would take us to get to the other side of our Milky Way Galaxy?"

"You have to be kidding?"

"No. sorry. Our minds really can't handle it. But WOW, it brings you back down to earth with a THUD. How very, very tiny we all are, and how short our lives."

Talon was silent for a moment. She was so animated with her explanation he couldn't help but grin. Mariah took her eye off the telescope and looked at him, sitting quietly in a chair right next to her. His head was down, and she could see a slight twirling of his thumbs.

"Talon?"

"How did your visit go with Al?" He couldn't avoid asking. He had to know if there was something to worry about – something Mariah might not be telling him.

"It was so nice to see him. Even a week can seem like forever and he said everything is doing well. I can't wait to get back to work. Is that what's bothering you?"

He knew, in a way, he was avoiding the real issue. "I guess I was just wondering more about how close we are instead of two stars. I almost feel like we are those 80 thousand years apart."

Rubbing her eyes, "Talon, ever since our first date I've had the feeling there is something you're not telling me. I even told Al that once. It was just a sense that you were holding something back, and it was affecting my choices. Then when you didn't show up for our dinner date, I didn't know what to think. Did you find someone else? Were you some kind of playboy who had grown tired of me? Did you leave town? I had no idea what was going on, and you never gave me so much as a hint about your past. So, I was really scared, Talon. Seriously."

Continuing to swirl his thumbs around the tips of his fingers, "Mariah, would you consider taking a trip with me?"

"What kind of trip?"

"To Defiance. It's the only way I can explain my past to you in a way that you will understand."

Getting down on the floor beside him she placed her head on his thigh, and after several moments said, "Sure. Yes. I'll go with you."

"Do you think you could leave this weekend?"

"Yes. Al will let me go. How long does it take to get there?"

"It's about five hours. We can stay in Breezewood."

"I know where Breezewood is. I've stopped there on the way to Cleveland. It's just past the halfway point."

"Yes. To Cleveland. Yes. That would be about right."

"Do you think we could go on up and visit my mom for a day or two?"

He thought for a moment. "We can spend one night in Breezewood. That will be enough time to show you what I want you to see. Then we can go up to Cleveland. Say we leave here on Saturday. We can spend Saturday night in Breezewood, but we'd have Saturday afternoon to see Defiance. Sunday on to Cleveland, getting there early afternoon. Spend Sunday night and Monday night with your mom and then head back Tuesday."

"That sounds good."

"I'd love to spend more time, but I've already missed so much work…"

"It's not a problem, Talon," she interrupted. "My mom will be thrilled to have us visit. I want to try to talk her into moving to Suffolk anyway. Maybe seeing you with me will encourage her to give it serious thought."

"Let's go tell Declan, Em and Al. We have three days before we leave so that gives us enough time to get organized."

"Are you sure Talon?" asked Declan, watching both Talon and Mariah.

"Yes. I could tell her, but it wouldn't have the same impact. She needs to see everything as I tell the story. I really think it's important, and it will tell her everything she should know," he looked at Mariah, "everything she needs to know to make her decision."

"What decision?" she stared at him.

"To stay or go."

"Oh!" Mariah's mouth snapped shut in silence.

"It might be more than you can handle. Regardless, I'll take you to Cleveland to see your mom. We'll make it up as we go, if we have to."

"Alright. That sounds like a plan then."

Declan looked at Emily, who nodded slightly.

"Then take the Lincoln, Talon," he offered. "Makes for a more comfortable drive."

Chapter 12

They arrived in Breezewood at 4, and by the time Talon got them checked into the Holiday Inn Express they both admitted they were starving. While there were a lot of fast food joints – it was after all where many east-west bound travelers picked up the Pennsylvania Turnpike – they decided to just walk next door to the Bob Evans restaurant.

"What are you thinking, Mariah?" Talon fidgeted with his napkin.

"I guess I'm just concerned about you."

Folding and unfolding his napkin, "And I guess I'm even more worried about you."

"Why?"

"I don't want to scare you off, and I might. Mariah, what I need to show you isn't pretty. I'll understand if you want to leave, at any time. Honestly. You've seen my *good* side and some of the *bad,* so now you need all the history."

Taking a deep breath and letting it out slowly, "I don't know what to expect, but unless you start showing me where you buried bodies, it will be alright."

"No bodies. I swear."

With a high noise level in the restaurant they ate in silence, often just glancing up to smile at each other. He wished they were sharing a room, but also knew that would be a huge mistake. There had almost been more hissing than kissing up to this point in their relationship, and there was no way he was going to jeopardize what he felt was his last chance with Mariah.

He took her hand as they returned to the hotel and was relieved when she didn't withdraw it.

"How about we plan to head out around 8 tomorrow morning. We can either grab a bite from the hotel continental breakfast or get breakfast at the travel plaza and I can fill up with gas."

"Sounds fine. Just tap on my door at 8 then."

Opting for the travel plaza they ate a good breakfast of bacon, eggs, and toast, then Mariah spent time checking out the gift store. Selecting a colorful jewelry box for her mom, and a bottle opener shaped like a hammer for her uncle, they began the tour after Talon filled the tank with gas.

Pulling up in front of his mother's home, "This was my address when I was a child."

"It's for sale."

"Yes, Declan took care of all that when we were up here for Bryce's funeral. He had it completely updated. There's nothing to see inside. It's empty, but," taking her hand, "we'll tour the yard."

As they began to walk, Talon heard his name being called.

"Talon. I'm sorry. I thought when I saw the car that Declan had come up to check on the house."

"Hi, Paula. May I introduce you to Mariah Rogers." Talon took Mariah's hand, pulling her in closer. "Mariah, this is Paula Steele, Emily's mother."

"I'm so glad to meet you, Mariah," greeted Paula. I've known the Seaton kids from birth, so you're in good hands. I don't want to interrupt, but if you have time and want a cup of coffee, feel free to stop over, anytime."

"Thanks, Paula," said Talon. We're just going to walk around for a few minutes then head on out for Cleveland to visit Mariah's mom, but we appreciate the offer."

Reaching up to give Talon a peck on his cheek, "You two have a wonderful trip, then. I hope to get a chance to know you better in the future, Mariah." She turned to head back to her house.

Talon turned to Mariah and grinned. "Betcha she'll be on the phone to Emily within two minutes, wondering who you are and why we're here. She's a super lady, Mariah." He chuckled.

Mariah squeezed his hand.

Exhaling, "Here goes my story." He looked down as he scraped the grass with the toe of his shoe. "I had three brothers, before Declan was born. Bryce. He's the one who just died. Braedon, one year younger than Bryce. And one named Cailen. Declan's son is named in his honor. Cailen, my brother, died when he was hit in the head by a baseball. He was 9 years old and wanted to pitch, so we let him. We had a bunch of guys in the neighborhood playing with us. Bryce hit a ball that hit Cailen in the head. He died in the hospital. Our lives came to a screeching halt. Our parents simply dropped out of life, quit caring for us, and it was so bad at home that Bryce and Braedon, who were 11 and 12, took off as soon as they could. I was 8. They left me behind. I was 12 when Declan was born, and he was basically not attended to very much. Somehow, he managed to live through the first few years, but as we got older, we had to fend for ourselves. I think Declan grew up on peanut butter and nothing much else unless his friends helped him out from their homes. But I hated him. I was angry, messed up, and starving myself. I felt he was taking what little help was available from our parents, including food, and a nice warm bed at night from me. Every time I tried to go into the house I was yelled at or swatted by my mom, so finally gave up trying to find warmth in the winter or food at any time. It was always hot in the summer – no air conditioning, so summers didn't matter much. By the time I was 15 I had spent most of Declan's life smacking him around, teasing him, and…"

Talon paused and squeezed Mariah's hand.

"And… taking every girl I could find behind the shack."

Pointing to the backyard, and the patch of dirt that was becoming a bed of weeds, "That's where the shack used to be." Taking in a long breath and blowing it out he glanced sideways at Mariah to see any reaction she might have upon hearing that part of his confession. But she was stoic. Almost thoughtful.

He continued. "Declan was always around. I knew it. I didn't care. But apparently, he knew what was going on behind that shed, and it tortured him to the point that he never dated. Not once." He paused again. "So, by the time I was 17 I had left home too. From then, to the age of 41…" he took a deep breath… "I lived in a shed behind a friend's house. No heat, no water, just a shed. 24 years of the shed. And… ah, and… I dragged woman after woman after woman into that shed, all willing to come, of course"

Turning he began leading her back to the car. So far, she hadn't indicated any emotion at all. Was that good, or bad? He had one more stop to make. She didn't say a word as they got in the car and Talon put it into gear.

Pulling up to a house about a mile down the road, "If you look behind this house you can see a small shed. I lived there. If it's like it was when I left it, about a year or so ago, there's a mattress in there, a children's table, pillow, blankets. A few odds and ends. Possibly a candle or my old flashlight. I'm sure all the food has been eaten by critters by now. No one paid any attention to me. They knew I'd never harm them, and it wasn't costing them anything for me to crash in their shed, so they just left me alone."

"Are you telling me that shed was your home for something like twenty years?" She gasped.

"Yeah. Pretty much."

"Jesus, Talon. That's horrible," she whispered. "How did you deal with no heat when it was below freezing?"

"My carpenter boss would let me crash in his little shop for the night. It had some heat. No facilities in there, cause it was just a small building behind his house, but it was nice for overnight sleeping. There were stores and places I could go to keep warm during the day, and, of course, I worked with the carpenter in that same building."

"Sounds like you had people who were willing to help you."

"The booze and the women were all I thought about. I had that part-time job with the local carpenter, and learned a lot from him, but it was mostly just a way to buy food and whatever kind of booze I could afford, or even manage to get to where it was sold. Beer, wine. The hard stuff, I drank whatever I could get. Anyway, when Dad died, and Declan arrived for the funeral all that changed. At first, I didn't think we'd get along at all, but in the end, after he heard the story about Cailen, he saved my life. Made me get into detox and counseling, then dragged me down to Suffolk for therapy."

"That clears up one thing I had wondered about."

"What's that."

"You never ordered anything alcoholic when we went out to eat."

"Can't. Never again."

"All that's not as bad as I was thinking, though, Talon."

"There's one more thing."

She locked eyes with him.

"I have at least one son. Maybe a couple of other children. Don't know for sure."

He watched to see if she was going to freak out.

Mariah held her breath, struggling to look at Talon with the energy that she usually found easily. She hadn't been expecting that. It was hard to comprehend the life that Talon was describing. It also concerned her that she felt his hand start shaking. Maybe he was giving her time to absorb what he had said so far? Or, maybe the worst was yet to come? She had to remain calm, or at least *appear* to remain calm.

After a lengthy pause, "Can I ask you a question, Mariah?"

"Of course," she replied, turning to look at him. She held his hand lightly.

"The night I went nuts, got drunk, that night. Ah, I drove by your place to see if I could talk to you. As I pulled up, I watched a man knock on your door and you let him inside. Was he someone, ah, special...? It's why I went... crazy."

"Oh, my God, Talon." She squeezed his hand with force. "He was the detective investigating my case. He wanted to go over everything again to see if I might have more information."

Turning his head toward Mariah, "Guess I'm not a very good example of someone who has changed," and turning his head away from her, "First I seem to stand you up. Then I don't understand why you won't talk to me, yet you have obviously been beat up. Then I make assumptions about the man..." heaving a gigantic sigh, he felt Mariah ease her grip on his hand.

"Talon, both of us made mistakes and both of us made assumptions that were invalid. Keep telling me your story, please."

"Well, I'll make it quick, like ripping off a bandage. Can't count the women. Became an alcoholic and minor drug abuser. And, I know I have one son. That's the sum total of my life."

Feeling a slight clench of her hand, all Talon could do was remain still. And pray. Her hand would shift and move a bit but did not disconnect from his.

"Tell me about your son."

Talon told her about Hunter, his mother, Sue, and that he had met her accidently while in Pennsylvania for Bryce's funeral. Opening his phone, he showed her a picture of Hunter.

"He's adorable and looks just like you." Her gaze shifted down and away from him.

"It won't be a problem. His mother is happily married, and Hunter has been adopted, so doesn't even carry my last name. I can live with that. But she did promise to keep me posted occasionally. However, with my history, it's always possible I have other children that I don't know about. Sue said she didn't think so, and she stays pretty much in the loop of Defiance rumor." Taking out his handkerchief and wiping his forehead, "Regardless, you need to know all of it. All my sordid past. Nothing more to learn. Dad died, and Declan pushed me into rehab. Declan tends to talk in 'actions and consequences' rather than outright advice. He leaves choices. He had never been told about Cailen's death, and when he was told, at Father's gathering, it was like the sun rose over the darkness of the night. Suddenly he understood everything. When I hurt my knee so badly, after rehab, he brought me down here to recover, and had Em do therapy for me. As you know, he has an entire section of the home with swimming pool and all kinds of exercise equipment. Then he married Em, and now here I am. Lived with them for quite some time until I got the business going and, ah, met you."

Shifting toward him she placed her head on his shoulder and brought her arm up across his chest. He was calm. Oddly. Like he was drained of everything and now had nothing left to expose. She closed her eyes, wishing she could say the same thing. In silence he brought his arm up to encircle Mariah, rubbing his hand up and down her arm, as if in comfort? Fear? Anxiety?

"So," she began, snapping her mind back to the present, "How did Declan and Emily meet then?"

"Rather interesting, that story. Seems while I was beating him up, around his age of 5 – something like that – he was fishing with a string on a stick on the river across from our house. Declan was always by himself. He never made any friends. Of course, now I understand why, and in today's world the child protection systems would have taken over... but I digress. So, he's fishing, and a little girl, about his age, walks up and tries to befriend him. He would have none of it. She quietly stands there and suddenly kisses him. She watched him all through their school years, but he never gave her so much as a look. Eventually he put himself through college, then moved here to Suffolk, and when he went back to Father's gathering there she was. Emily had never stopped loving him, but this time he did take small notice. She had just taken a job in Chesapeake, so their paths were going to cross often, since she's a therapist and he deals in items that they use. Ultimately, he figured out he loved her, after he almost lost her, and they've been the happiest two people on earth ever since. Well, I guess they'd be happier if I could quit messing up all the time."

He felt her giggling. "What?"

"You. Do you want help in your efforts to quit messing up all the time?"

"You volunteering?"

"If you like."

"Oh, I like."

"Okay," and lifting her head she turned his chin down and gave him a kiss. It was hard to let that kiss go.

"I've never uttered these words to anyone before, but I love you, Mariah."

Her eyes twinkled. "And I do believe I love you right back." *And, please, God, let him continue to love me when he finds out my secret past.*

Running his fingers through her hair, "Then let's get some lunch back in Breezewood, and head to Cleveland."

"My thoughts, exactly."

134

Chapter 13

Lisa's home was a small, three-bedroom ranch with brick facing and a well-manicured lawn.

"Mom and Dad were raised in Cleveland, but after he got out of the Navy they just decided to stay in Virginia. After he died, she thought she'd move back here, but I've never figured out why. Who wants to live in a place where you have to shovel snow? And I was going to stay in Suffolk. Always wondered about that."

"Hard to say, naturally. Maybe she was trying to recapture her youth. Are there other relatives up here?"

"That's probably it. She has a brother and sister up here. I think she might even be living in the house that *her* parents owned. Grandmother died around that time. I went to the funeral, but you know how it is when you're in your twenties and rushing around living your own life."

"Can't say that anything like that ever happened to *me,* but I understand what you are saying."

The door opened and her mother rushed out and grabbed her in a hug.

"Mom, this is Talon. I wanted you to meet him."

Lisa opened her arms and Talon accepted the hug. "You are so kind to bring Mariah up to visit me. I'm thrilled to meet you. Come on into the house. I've made some soup and sandwiches for you."

Talon liked what he saw. Not only did he immediately love Lisa, but her home was warm and comfortable. The living room was just big enough for a couch and two chairs, accompanied by end tables. A nice sized TV was placed so that anyone could see it from where they were seated. Following Lisa into the kitchen both he and Mariah sat down at the table while Lisa spooned soup into bowls.

"I've missed you so much, Mariah," she said, sitting down with them. "I have to admit seeing all the marks on your body make me cringe, but you said you are alright now."

"I am Mom. There's still some apprehension, but the physical scars are healing. The doctors said it would just take a while."

"I just thank God those people showed up when they did and scared him away."

Sipping her soup, "This is good Mom. I'd forgotten how good." She sipped another spoonful. "This is one of Mom's special soups, Talon. It's potato soup with added celery, onion and green pepper, and of course the hot dogs, cut up. Always was one of my favorites growing up." She hoped this was an effective change of subject. She wasn't anxious to get into the night of horror again, and she had clearly explained all of it to her mom on the phone, after she'd gotten home from the hospital.

"I can see why," nodded Talon. "And grilled cheese sandwiches are my favorite."

Lisa smiled. "I know you're only here for two days, but I'll love every minute of it," she said.

"Mom, I want you to start thinking about moving back to Suffolk. Admit it. You know more people down there than you do here. Uncle Al would be thrilled to have you back. He'd probably even put you to work. Hard to get competent help, even just to answer the phone," she snuck a glance toward Talon. "Al has me doing so much site supervising it's hard for me to stick around the office. What say you?"

"Truthfully, Mariah?"

"Yes, Mom. Truthfully."

I don't really see John and Mae as much as I thought I would. John and Sara are even planning a move to Florida, and Mae has always been distant to all of us. I am giving thoughts to getting back with that daughter of mine down in Suffolk, though," she reached over and patted her daughter's hand.

"Oh, MOM! That would be so spectacular."

"I'm thinking about it. No promises."

Wandering around the living room he picked up assorted pictures and studied at them. Bringing one into the kitchen, where Mariah remained with her mom, "Mariah, is this a picture of your brother's family?"

Taking the picture from his hand she glanced at her mom and then said, "Why, yes. It's my brother Mike, his wife Sandy and their son."

"Nice looking family," admired Talon. "We'll have to go visit them sometime." Turning he took the picture back and headed to return it to the living room. He heard Lisa's voice shift to a whisper, "Have you told him about Ryan yet, Mariah?"

He didn't hear her reply, it was whispered too softly. He'd have to ask her about Ryan when he got the chance.

The tour of the rest of the house was short. Three small bedrooms and one bath. That was it. Talon brought in the luggage, putting Mariah's in the pink bedroom, and his in the blue. Seemed rather obvious to him, and Mariah could only laugh. This was the second pink bedroom Talon had been subjected to. Did all women have pink bedrooms, he wondered. They spent the rest of the day catching up and getting to know each other.

Even though the stay was short Lisa had managed to drag them to the South East Harley- Davidson restaurant for a hamburger lunch the next day. Despite having no interest in motorcycles, Talon was fascinated by the operation. A gift shop with several HOGS on display was clean and brightly lit. Adjacent to it was a small cafeteria. And the best hamburger he'd eaten in years.

"Don't even think about it," Mariah said, watching as Talon ran his fingers over the largest HOG in the display room.

He laughed. "Nah. Not to worry. I'd crash it in less than a mile."

"And in Ohio they don't even have to wear helmets. Most don't. They are known as organ donors," added Lisa.

"EW," moaned Mariah. "Geeze, Mom. Don't need that graphic in my head."

Settling back into the car, Lisa asked them if they would go chair shopping with her. "I need to get a more comfortable chair to sit in, and sure could use the advice of one who know a lot about constructing them," she said.

"I don't make chairs right now, Lisa, but I do know construction, so I'm sure I could be of some assistance. The carpenter I worked with in Defiance once told me he was asked to reupholster a chair. He took the old fabric and stuffing off, then was shocked to see the rest of the chair was nothing but Styrofoam. Said there wasn't a toothpicks worth of wood in it."

"I guess it would be hard to figure out what's under all that fabric," she said.

"True, but sometimes if you tilt the chair back and look under it you can see part of what it's made of. That's especially true of recliners."

By the third furniture store Lisa had decided on the chair she wanted, and Talon was comfortable that it wasn't made of Styrofoam. The salesman assured them there was real wood under the microfiber fabric. Delivery would take two weeks, since it was a special order, but they would unbox it, place it in the room, make sure it worked well, and then remove the old chair.

Insisting that they also eat dinner out, Lisa named a favorite rib restaurant in a nearby shopping center, and they all agreed that a meal of baby back ribs would be good.

Licking BBQ sauce off her fingers, "Mom, really, please consider moving back to Suffolk. I'll come up and help you move."

"There's a good chance, Mariah. With my brother moving and my lack of connection to my sister, I'd sure rather be with you. The plus is there's almost never any snow in Suffolk."

"Good. The sooner the better," Mariah smiled.

Tired from the long day, Talon excused himself and went to bed early, wanting to give Mariah and her mom time to talk.

Sitting in the kitchen with cups of cocoa in front of them, "Do you love him, Mariah?"

"I do, Mom. He's had a rough life. He's a recovering alcoholic, but the kindest, sweetest man I've ever met."

"And certainly not hard to look at," mused her mom with a twinkle in her eye.

Mariah blushed. "He takes my breath away."

"I like him, Mariah. And the way he looks at you... your dad used to look at me that same way. I miss him so much."

"I know Mom. I do too."

They left too soon for both of them. With a promise to return another time, for a much longer visit, they headed down the road to return to Virginia.

Turning onto the onramp for the Ohio Turnpike, "A penny for your thoughts," he said, as he stopped to pick up the toll ticket.

"I'm happy, Talon. You've been open and honest with me, and no one could ask for more."

Merging into the eastbound traffic, he began to whistle.

"Would you mind if I took a nap?" asked Mariah. "Mom and I stayed up until after midnight catching up, and I think I've convinced her to move back to Suffolk. She wants me to start looking for a place for her to live, like a small apartment or condo. She doesn't want a house anymore."

"I know you'd love to have her near you," said Talon, "so if you need any help just let me know. And sure, take a nap. These cars are made for that kind of comfort."

It was almost dark when he dropped Mariah off at her home.

"I know you slept most of the way home, but do get a good night's sleep," he advised. "We both have to work tomorrow."

She burst out laughing. "Yes, that will be a change for us, won't it?"

He rolled her luggage into her house, then pulled her toward him for a hug. With his cheek resting against hers, "Oh, Mariah, you have no idea how much you mean to me." Pulling back, he brushed her lips with his. "Friday night?"

"Yes. It's a date."

He couldn't keep the excitement to himself, and he suspected Declan and Emily were flat out dying to know what had transpired in those past few days. One quick call to be sure they were home and he was on his way. His only question was about someone named Ryan. An ex-husband? Boyfriend? He was a bit confused as to why she hadn't said anything to him about him, especially since he had been so open and honest with her about his past. But maybe this was a current situation? He had no idea.

Emily stood just inside the door and handed Cailen to him. "We're about to put him to bed, but I thought you'd like to see him."

Snatching him from Emily's arms, "Hey, Buddy. UP we go," as he lifted him to the ceiling, "and DOWN we come," as he dipped him toward the floor. Cailen giggled.

Talon's smile was immense, and just then Declan came into the room. Emily could visibly see Declan relax. Talon continued swinging Cailen around the room. "Nothing beats a giggling kid," he said.

Looking back over at Em and Declan, "What?"

Declan rubbed his chin, "Well, we got a call while you two were wandering around Pennsylvania and Ohio. What I didn't tell you before, Talon, was that the police had borrowed a couple of off-duty troopers from the State Police. They came into the pub every night and sat there for 3-4 hours, pretending to be part of the group. When Mariah's assailant wandered in, the barkeep signaled, and they had him in custody in a split second. Turns out he's, ah, done this many times and had just gotten out of prison the week before. He's on his way back for sure, and we're going to try to get a confession, so Mariah won't have to appear for any trial. It shouldn't be too hard. They have the DNA from where she scratched him, and of course the bartender would testify that he watched him follow her out of the pub."

Still holding Cailen, Talon took his phone out of his pocket and quickly called Mariah.

"Guess what!" he teased her.

"You couldn't wait to go see Cailen," she guessed.

"Well, that too, but they got the guy that assaulted you, Mariah."

Declan and Emily could hear the squeal as Talon held the phone away from his ear.

"Can I take you to dinner tomorrow night, to celebrate? Like we used to do. Soda's at Shamrock Pub?"

"I'd love it. Now, I'd like to go call Uncle Al and let him know."

Putting Cailen back into his mother's arms, "I'm going to go back to work tomorrow, Declan."

"I think that's the best thing you can do, Talon."

"It seems like things are starting to work out alright," Talon looked at both of them.

"Then you had a nice trip!" It was a statement from Emily, not a question.

"Yes. Very nice. I think Mariah accepted my past…" he paused. "And I want to share the only part of my story that you don't already know." His eyes shifted back and forth between them.

While Emily bounced Cailen in her arms, Declan stood stock still.

"When I was up there for Bryce's funeral I ran into, ah, one of my former lady friends."

Proceeding with the rest of the story he took out his phone and showed them the picture he had of Hunter. "I told Sue if he's interested when he gets older, she can tell him who his real dad is. Anyway. I don't think I have any other kids but may never know. Sue and Hunter will never be any problem though."

Emily and Declan gazed at each other, then said at the same time. "Good!"

"Maybe now we can all move forward," suggested Talon.

"Great idea," agreed Emily, while Declan reached over and shook Talon's hand. "But," added Emily, "I sense a bit of reticence."

Talon put a hand on top of his head, "I promised you two I'd never keep something from you again, and I won't. It's just a feeling, but twice now I've overheard conversations that cause me some concern. The first was when Al came here to visit Mariah, and I heard him ask, 'have you told him yet.,' or words to that effect. Then her mom asked her if she had told me about someone named Ryan." Bringing his hand down, "I haven't said anything to her. I was never eavesdropping but just overheard it. I was kinda hoping she'd open up about it on the way home, but all she wanted to do was sleep."

Emily sat down and cradled Cailen on her lap. "Then you'll have to ask her, Talon. You've been more than fair with telling her everything, and she should feel just as comfortable telling you what you should know."

Declan nodded his head. "Maybe it should be the topic of conversation on your next date," he suggested.

"Tomorrow night... okay... Yes... okay," agreed Talon.

Chapter 14

Arms loaded with boxes of donuts Talon walked into his office. Anna looked up at the noise and went into shock, recovered, squealed, then jumped up and gave him a gigantic hug.

"Oh, my *gosh*, Talon, it's so good to see you. Aaron and Jacob have asked about you every day, but we didn't want to bother Declan. We've been so worried about you. Are you okay now? Have you seen Mariah? How is she…?"

"WHOA!" Smiled Talon. "Alright. Good to see you, too. Declan would not have minded any calls. I'm grateful that you were concerned. I'm fine now. Yes, I've seen Mariah. She's fine too. Did that cover all the questions?"

Opening a donut box and selecting one of the cream donuts, she took a bite and licked her fingers. "Oh, *so* good. I'll just eat while you go tell the guys you are here and to get some donuts before I eat them all."

Walking into the shop he was shocked! Aaron and Jacob were moving at double pace it seemed. Cabinets were all over the place, in various stages of finishing. There were, apparently, some new hires, as he counted eight other Amish gentlemen hard at work.

Shaking hands and answering questions all around, he finally narrowed the group down to just Aaron and Jacob.

"Looks like you guys didn't even miss me. I take a couple days off and the place explodes with cabinets."

"Al brought in another customer. Offices. We're booming and might have to hire even more help."

"You let me know what you need, and I'll make it happen. Or, more likely, I'll let YOU keep making it happen. You are incredible. Both of you. I'll have to double your salaries at this rate?"

"We'd never object to that, Talon," grinned Jacob.

"There are donuts in the office that Anna is doing her best to eat before all of you get there…"

He didn't need to say any more.

The rest of the day went smoothly. He went over the books and orders with Anna. "Did you hear I just might have to double your salary?"

"Yes. I but I really don't do that much work. I love my job and everyone I work with."

"We're family. You – all of you – kept me afloat. I didn't have to worry that I would lose the business. That can't be repaid. But I can try," he chuckled.

"I'm glad Mariah is okay Al told us what happened."

"She's fine now, and they caught the guy, so no more worries. I'm having dinner with her tonight."

Anna smiled. "Good, very good."

Both Mariah and Talon had returned to their respective residences to get ready for dinner, and when Talon drove up to knock on her door, she opened it and pulled him in for a kiss. "I missed you today."

"Oh, woman. You are all I've thought about today."

"The pub?"

"The pub!"

Arriving, as was their preference, ahead of the busy hour, they sat down at their favorite table. The evening went like every other time they had been there, except the wait and bar staff were thrilled to see them. Ordering their usual they ate, telling jokes, making plans for the next week, talking about Declan and his family, and just looking into each other's eyes.

Returning from the bathroom Mariah couldn't help but notice that Talon seemed lost in thought. "You seem so far away, Talon. Are you alright?"

Helping her on with her jacket, "I do need to ask you about something."

"Sure."

Once in the car he started the engine and turned into the street.

"What did you want to ask?" she reached over and touched his hand.

Removing his hand from beneath Mariah's, he gulped. "Who is Ryan?"

From his peripheral view he saw her stiffen and catch her breath. Several seconds passed before she uttered softly, "He's my son, Talon. I was seventeen when he was born. When his father found out I was pregnant he vanished. He was nineteen and we'd been dating for several months. My parents supported me throughout. I knew my brother and his wife could never have children and they were beyond thrilled to adopt my son. He knows he has two mothers. We aren't keeping any secrets from him."

He was pulling into her driveway and turned off the engine. He turned to look at her. Tears were streaming down her face and her fear was obvious.

"Please don't hate me Talon. I'm so sorry. You've been open and honest with me and I was just so afraid once you knew about Ryan you'd cut and run like his father did. It's been ten years and I have no idea where he is, and he's never tried to contact us."

Talon dropped his arms from the steering wheel to his lap and put his head back onto the head rest.

"How did you know?" she asked.

"I heard Al ask you if you had told me something, and then your mother asked almost the same thing but used the name Ryan. I kept hoping you trusted me enough to tell me about him. I've wondered if he was an ex-husband or current boyfriend. It hurts that you have so little faith in me."

"I'm so very sorry, Talon. I was so scared you couldn't handle knowing about him."

Talon didn't move, he just nodded. When he didn't say anything for a good minute Mariah opened her car door, got out, and walked into her house.

Talon started the car and drove away.

Her heart sank when she heard his car start. She watched the lights come on, shine through her window and play against the wall of the room, then vanish. Sobbing she walked into her bedroom and flopped onto the bed. *You were right to worry, Mariah. You've been stupid to think you could ever have another relationship. He didn't say anything, he just drove away. That was as good a rejection as any other.* She knew she would never stop loving him. Her dreams were going to be sad.

Ringing the doorbell, Talon waited. When the door opened, he looked at Emily, who knew at once that something was wrong.

"Oh, no, Talon. Come in."

"Declan home?" he asked.

"No. I'll get the coffee."

Following her into the kitchen, he waited until she asked, "Tell me what's wrong, Talon."

Talon told her about Mariah's son, and what had happened.

"How do you feel about it? What are you thinking?"

"I'm just so hurt, Em. There's just no reason for her not to have told me upfront. I did everything in my power to make sure she knew all about my past, so she could make decisions accordingly. I thought we were alright, but she didn't trust me enough."

"Are you angry?"

"Yes. I guess I feel so hurt that I feel angry too. It stung. I just shut down and couldn't even say anything to her. It's not that she has a child. I keep thinking it's like my own story but backwards, and she was with a guy like me who just did shallow relationships and then ran when the going got real."

"Then what is it?"

"She didn't believe in me. Didn't trust me."

"Do you want to salvage the relationship?"

"I guess the balls in her court, Em."

"Hmm. Seems more to me like it's in both courts at the same time. She's probably thinking you have rejected her now, so she'll have to back off and get back to the life she had before she met you. You have to decide if you love her enough to get past the pain of feeling she didn't trust you. If you two can't find a way to talk it all out then you'll both spend your lives apart, regretting that you didn't at least try to communicate your feelings to each other."

He nodded. "I'll think about it, Em. I hear what you're saying." Standing to leave, "How's Cailen doing?"

"He's fine. Listen. Why don't you spend the night? Your room is still ready, and Declan will be home soon."

"I appreciate it, Em, but I'll just go home. I promise. No bars."

"Come back if you change your mind, okay?"

Squeezing her hand and placing a quick kiss on her cheek, "Okay. And thanks."

It took a week to sort through all his emotions. He was surprised, but thankful, that no one at work asked him why he was so quiet. Keeping busy was the best outlet to keep his mind from overthinking his problems. There was no question that he loved her. He even knew he wanted to marry her. But if she couldn't trust him... if she was afraid to tell him something... that just wasn't good. It wouldn't work. He couldn't fathom how she thought she could manage keeping it a secret forever. Would she have married him and then made her brother, sister-in-law, and son swear to keep her secret? That was just stupid. She had said her son knew she was his mother and he had two mothers. So why try to hide it all from him? Did she really think so little of him? He did have to smile though. Emily called him at least once a day to see how he was doing. It was nice to be thought of and it meant a lot to him.

She was wrong and she knew it. She hadn't heard from him in a week and she didn't blame him. How could she think he wouldn't understand? He had to have been terrified to share all his past life with her. Her life was so simple compared to his. She'd had family support at every turn and had never gone hungry in her life.

Even the memories of Ryan's father weren't all that bad anymore. After all these years she knew he'd never show up or bother her for any information about his child. She doubted he even knew he had a son. His parents had moved so there wasn't even anyone left to find. The best part was being able to watch her son grow into a man. Mike and Sandy were doing an outstanding job raising him, and she always drove up to Richmond for his birthdays and Christmas. He did well in school, loved sports, played a clarinet, and best of all he loved to read. Getting him books was an easy gift for him. And then it hit her. An idea that just might work. The telescope had worked. Maybe this next idea would work too. She would take care of it tomorrow.

"You have another package in the office," Anna paged.
"Did we order something special?" he inquired.
"This is something personal for you."

Turning off the saw and dusting off the sawdust, he headed to the office. Anna handed him a small box. Seeing the return address his hands started to shake.

"Why don't you take it to your private office to open it," she suggested.

He hesitated. Then took the utility knife and swiped it across the seal. Slowly opening the flaps, he could barely breathe. Listing the tissue off the top he was stunned. It was a toy or something. He pulled it out of the box and set it on the counter, staring at it.

"Oh, my God," exclaimed Anna. "This is so incredible…" Talon was surprised to see tears flowing down her cheeks.

"I don't understand, Anna. It's just a toy."

"Oh, Talon. You have no idea. This is a Velveteen Rabbit Gift set." She grabbed a tissue and started wiping tears from her cheeks.

"Okay," he said, turning the box around and around and looking at the little stuffed rabbit inside and the book that came with it.

"Take it and go home and read the book. Read it two or three times. It's not long. And, oh my God," she started crying again, "What an incredibly perfect thing to send to you."

"Alright. But you gotta quit the crying stuff. I'll read it tonight."

He was overwhelmed. After the fourth reading he put the book down and picked up the little stuffed rabbit. "Ah, little rabbit. Nice and shiny and new at birth, then worn down to a frazzle, except you lost your fur because you were loved, while I lost mine because I wasn't. Well, maybe Mariah is trying to tell me that you are brand new, just as I am brand new in my changed life, and maybe she wants to be the one to be responsible for wearing down my new fur coat. What say you?" he whispered, holding the plush rabbit up in front of his face and running his hand down its soft exterior. "Maybe I should name you 'Defiant" to always remind me of what I used to be and what I can now become." He stood, put the rabbit down on the counter, and picked up his phone to send a message to Mariah. Maybe she'd agree to dinner this coming weekend.

Dinner finished; Mariah was surprised to see the wait staff bringing two flutes of what appeared to be Champagne. At the same time the door to the pub opened, and at the POP of the bubbly Mariah felt a tap on her shoulder. Turning she burst into tears. "Oh, My God. Dear Lord. MOM!"

Standing behind her Max was grinning from ear to ear. "Best delivery I ever made, Miss Mariah!"

Mariah stood up and grabbed her mom for a huge hug. "Oh, MOM, it doesn't get any better than this. Who did this?"

"Goodness, Mariah, Talon called me, and I was on the next plane."

Mariah started to cry. "It's so good to see you, Mom. Does that mean you might move back down here?"

"It's seriously on my list of things to do, Mariah. Part of this trip will be apartment or condo hunting."

"Sit, Sit..." Talon stood and offered his seat to Mariah's mom. Taking her hand, "I'm so happy you could make it."

"Oh, Talon I am glad to see you again. I'm thrilled you called me."

"Will there be any further need for me, sir?" asked Max.

"No, but you are welcome to pull up a chair and have a glass of ginger ale with us."

As quickly as they could the wait staff rushed to bring more chairs to the table.

Turning toward him, Mariah chimed in, "Please do stay, Max. We would love to have you join us."

"As you wish, Miss Mariah!"

Seeing her mother's quizzical look, "It's a southern thing Mom. You must have forgotten your southern manners!" Everyone grinned.

The door opened and Declan and Emily walked in, with Al not far behind them.

"Oh, my gosh, it's a party," Mariah said, clapping her hands.

As introductions were being made the restaurant staff was busy rearranging tables to accommodate the added customers. Talon had assured them it would be worth whatever they had to do to have this chance to bring Mariah back into his life.

Finally, everyone was seated. Several had flutes of champagne and others, like Talon, Mariah, and Em filled their classes with ginger ale.

"Folks," began Talon, "Before I offer the toast, there's one last thing."

All eyes turned toward Talon, who had risen from the booth and was now kneeling down in front of Mariah. The shock on her face was exactly what he was waiting to see. Looking up at her, "Mariah Rogers. I know I haven't given you a lot of time to think things through, but would you do me the honor of becoming my wife?"

Stunned, Mariah could only gasp as she saw the gorgeous two carat diamond ring, gently being held in Talon's hands. She noticed his hands begin to shake a bit, so she reached down and cupped them in her hands. Leaning down she whispered "yes," with an immediate gentle kiss.

The pub exploded in cheers, and as he rose to kiss Mariah back, he observed Aaron, Jacob and Anna had entered the pub without his noticing.

"Don't worry. It's ginger ale," he said to them, his smile so broad it almost lit up the room. "But I would like to toast what we have been through and where we are going if that's alright with you."

"Everyone held up their glasses and cheered." They all locked eyes and Talon, arms around Mariah, who added very shyly, "No more bad times, only good times." Clinking glasses and tasting the ginger ale, Mariah looked at Talon, who seemed to be lost in thought.

"Talon? Are you alright?"

"I guess I just can't believe how lucky I am to have a past like mine and convince a wonderful woman like you to marry me."

"Oh, Talon. If you only knew. That first day when you came through the shop door, I could not believe that I was staring at the most breathtaking man I had ever seen. And when you shook my hand it was all I could do to keep standing."

Talon grinned. "Interesting. Same thing happened to me. You were way too gorgeous to want to have anything to do with me."

Holding the ring up for everyone to see, Mariah beamed, "This is the most wonderful day of my life. You, my mom, the whole family to share it all with. My heart is so full."

"I love you, Mariah," said Talon.

"And I love you as well, Talon. But one thing I think I finally figured out." Taking Talon's hand, she walked him across the room, and grabbed Al by the shirt tail. "Dear Uncle Al set us up. There was really no reason why I had to come to your shop to see if delivery could be earlier. That could have been done with a phone call. Yes. I'll have to thank him for that," she said, as she punched his shoulder! Al just grinned back at her, leaned down and kissed her forehead, then gave her a big hug.

With the ginger ale gone Declan made it clear that Lisa would have a room in the East wing. Whispering in Emily's ear, Mariah asked if they would be offended if her mom stayed with her, and the house she used to live in. When her parents had moved to Cleveland, she had taken over the house, and it sure had plenty of space!

"Of course not. That's a much better idea. We just want Lisa to know she is always welcome in our home."

"Mom," Mariah said, turning to find Lisa in the crowd that had gathered.

Finally, "You come home with me. I know you'll love being back in the old house, and I'll even let you have the master bedroom back for your stay!" She laughed, "Talon will deliver us, and we can start wedding planning."

Declan, Emily, and Max, left together, while Al headed for his truck to drive home. Hugging his niece, "You have no idea how thrilled I am that you and Talon were able to work all this out."

"Not as much as we are, Uncle. And listen, I don't know how long Mom will be here, but please try to take some time out to spend with us – or take her to dinner. You're still her favorite brother-in-law, you know."

Giving her a gentle hug, "Funny niece. I'm her only brother-in-law. Don't worry. I'll make myself more than a little bit available!"

Once inside the car, Talon couldn't get a word in edgewise for all the chatter between Mariah and Lisa. He loved every single second of it.

"Mom, listen. No wedding until all the black and blue and cuts have healed. I could see you were shocked that I still have some scars – I wasn't *exactly* honest with you when I called after I got out of the hospital the first time, but you know I'm fine now and just need to heal a bit. The wounds get lighter every day. How long can you stay?"

"Ask Talon. It's his ticket," she grinned.

"Ticket is unlimited stay." Talon managed to say.

"Oh, Mom, we can go wedding dress shopping, and at least *start* on the wedding plans. It really won't be too hard, as I want a very small wedding. Unless of course, Talon disagrees." She paused. She knew he was listening to every word.

"Small is perfect for me. Just family and my work gang. They'd be very upset if they missed the result of all the stuff they watched me go through."

"Family and close friends, then, Mom. Figure out if there's anyone you want to invite. And Mom, think about how soon you'll be moving back here? I know you liked Cleveland, but there really isn't anything up there for you now?"

"No, honey, no more reason to stay in Cleveland. And trust me. I'll not miss the snow. If this is where you are going to be then I want to be close. We can see what's available in the housing market."

"Well, you can have the house back! I'll move in with Talon as soon as we find a nice place together."

"Hm. I don't think I want the stress of taking care of a house anymore. I need maintenance free at my age."

"We can find you something for sure."

"What do the doctors say as far as your healing?"

"Probably another two or three weeks before the scars and all the black and blue are gone. I'm really only concerned with my face."

Talon, hearing a small piece of silence, "We can go house hunting tomorrow?"

They both laughed. "Nothing like wanting you all to himself," observed Lisa.

"Can you blame me?" teased Talon, looking in the rear-view mirror. This chauffer stuff was harder than he realized. Talking to people in the back seat needed an intercom!!!

Pulling up to Mariah's he opened the back door, helping Lisa out, then scrambled to the other side to help Mariah out.

"I'll give you tomorrow with your mom, and I'll go catch up on my business. Then we shop for a house, okay? And you can set the date, so we can get a place and pastor and cake and whatever you want for the wedding."

"Yes, and yes. Okay," she burst out laughing. "But we can text! We can also discuss just keeping the house I'm already in rather than get something new for us. Your apartment is too small, and mom doesn't want a house anymore, but we can talk about all the options."

"Absolutely!"

Watching until they were safely into the house, he slowly backed out of the driveway and headed to his own apartment. Tonight, he would sleep.

Epilog

The wedding was small, but just what Mariah wanted. Talon couldn't have cared less. All he was interested in was the end result. With Declan as his Best Man, Mariah asked Emily to be her Matron of Honor. The guests, other than family, were the staff of Talon's shop, Al, and the owner of the pub. Mariah was thrilled to have her brother, sister-in-law, and son, Ryan there, to support her and meet Talon. God did not make days any better than this.

The weather was perfect, and Emily had taken control of the decorations and settings for the back-yard nuptials, along with a very nice reception afterwards. When Declan and Emily offered their back yard for the wedding, with a reception in the house afterward, Talon and Mariah couldn't say 'no.' A nice 'side' event would be looking at the sky from the observatory telescope, as the wedding was planned for sunset. The men were in suits and Mariah wore a beautiful white, floor length gown, with a sweetheart neckline, decorated with sequins and pearls. She wore her hair down, with a beautiful veil flowing behind. As the veil was caught in the slight breeze, the gown's sequins glistened, reflecting the sun's setting glow.

Talon held his breath. And when he saw her, he couldn't help but sense the tears forming in his eyes. How lucky could one man, with his past life, get? As much as he had abused Declan the man had saved his life on more than one occasion. This day wasn't just a marriage, it was a promise of a future, and one he wouldn't betray ever again.

Holding hands and exchanging rings he thanked God for leading him to this place in life. And kissing his bride, as she became Mrs. Talon Seaton, he put his feet rock solid on earth.

If ever there was a hit of a reception it was the observatory. Everyone was not only surprised but thrilled. Declan finally had to kick everyone out at midnight, with a promise to hold an "observatory" party in the very near future.

Lisa was leaving in three days to begin packing up to move back to Suffolk. She found a great deal! Talon would move into the house with Mariah and she would take Talon's old apartment. It was a good start. With a lot of work, he would soon be able to prove to Declan that he was worth all the effort Declan and Emily had taken to save him.

But, to Talon, one thing stood out above all else. When Mariah introduced him to her brother and his family, Ryan took his hand and exclaimed, "I've loved having two moms. Now I'll have two dads. Can't beat that at all."

Talon thought his heart would burst.

But all that would wait. A honeymoon in Austria, deep in the Alps, would keep them out of town for ten days.

Made in the USA
Middletown, DE
23 March 2020